Inquire Within

Short
Fictions

Jan Fancy Hull

Cover image: *The Heart of the Matter,* sculptor Beverley McInnes; photo by Kesha McInnes
Cover design: Rebekah Wetmore
Author's photo: Betty Meredith
Editor: Andrew Wetmore
ISBN: 978-1-990187-26-1
First edition June, 2022

MOOSE HOUSE
PUBLICATIONS

2475 Perotte Road
Annapolis County, NS
B0S 1A0

moosehousepress.com
info@moosehousepress.com

We live and work in Mi'kma'ki, the ancestral and unceded territory of the Mi'kmaw people. This territory is covered by the "Treaties of Peace and Friendship" which Mi'kmaw and Wolastoqiyik (Maliseet) people first signed with the British Crown in 1725. The treaties did not deal with surrender of lands and resources but in fact recognized Mi'kmaw and Wolastoqiyik (Maliseet) title and established the rules for what was to be an ongoing relationship between nations. We are all Treaty people.

Also by Jan Fancy Hull

Where's Home?

The Church of Little Bo Peep and other stories

The Tim Brown Mysteries

January: Code

February: Curious

March: Enigma (coming soon)

...all from Moose House Publications

Why should we not calmly and patiently
review our own thoughts?
– Plato

These stories are dedicated to those who are
curious about the private thoughts of others,
and brave enough to examine their own.

Introduction

First to arrive in my imagination was the dream-seller. I was driving at night, telling myself this story out loud to help the miles go by. I asked to buy one of her dreams, but she declined. She would sell me my own dream, if I would declare it. That got my attention.

This dream-seller holds a mirror to her clients to help them understand their desires, and she assesses whatever fee she judges will motivate them. That's smart. Our dreams frequently stay in dreamland because there's no sharp stick, no impetus to get on with it. Her strength is in her powerful belief in her clients' abilities, coupled with her refusal to accept excuses. It's a kind of love, but it's tough.

I recognize myself in each person I've sketched herein: the man who just wants to punch people in the nose, the writer who thinks musicians have it easy, the woman who protects herself by judging others, the unorthodox cleric.

I've explored my own thoughts, as Plato advised. Perhaps these stories will do that for you, too. At least, I hope they'll entertain you.

-jfh

This is a work of fiction. The author has created the characters, conversations, interactions, and events; and any resemblance of any character to any real person is coincidental.

Contents

Jan Fancy Hull

Suite 101: The Interrogator

I gotta tell you, it completely blew me away, the way things went down that time when I lost my voice. I'm okay now, of course. I've fully recovered, thanks for asking. But sometimes I stop talking on purpose now. It's a useful tool.

I came down with this sore throat, see. A fairly ferocious sore throat, in fact. The doc said it was the worst case she'd seen—and I'm here to tell you she wasn't exaggerating. One minute you're talking and everything is as it should be. And then—bam!—it hits you like a bullet at close range.

You know what it felt like? It felt like someone crept up behind me and stuck their thumbs in my ears and their fingers in my eyes while tightening a hot wire around my throat. Not gently, either. You try that sometime.

So this throat bug caught me just as I was getting on to something while I was interviewing this creep —oh, sorry, I guess I didn't explain that I'm a PI, a private eye, as civilians call us, but in my case the "eye" means interrogator, not investigator.

I *was* in investigations, but I ran into a little trouble when I maybe crossed some line that was blown way out of proportion by some jumped-up little legal beagle who didn't know the score. Which shouldn't matter if you're taking down one of this city's drug-dealing low-lifes. Anyway, I made what the bureaucrats call a CLM—a Career-Limiting Move.

So they told me to cease and desist the investigations role. That's what the judge called it, a role. What's he think I am, an actor in his little amateur theatre? He likes to do his thing out at the Frog Pond Playhouse, thinks he's a big frog, but that's a pretty small pond. I had bigger fish I was trying to fry.

But what bothered me and the decent members of the police force was that I was right, and the weasel —that's the weasel drug dealer, not M'Lud the Judge —got off because they had to throw out my evidence. The thing is, I'm good at what I do. Did. Which was private investigations.

Most people don't know this, but sometimes even the officials hire PIs to check things out for them, where it wouldn't be good for them to be seen poking around themselves. Hell, they'd hire a little old lady that paints flowers if they were reasonably certain she'd be safe and it meant they could bust more of these creeps. Bet she'd be good at it, too.

Anyway, after all that shinola went down, I was sitting home, nursing my wounded pride and wondering if maybe I should buy a franchise, like home inspections or something like that. It's bird work, but it looks like work. I needed at least to appear to work.

Those clever, clever tax people at Canada Revenue

want to see effort go out before they see money go in your bank account, and I've a little money comes in from time to time, all legit of course, no harm to anyone, but not something those eraser-heads need to know the details of.

So, I was sitting home feeling pissed at certain specific elements of the world, when I got a surprise visit from some of our city's finest. In street clothes and an unmarked car, can you imagine? If I've told them once, I've told them a hundred times: that just screams 'cop'. Better they should drive right up in uniforms in a cruiser, even with the roof lights running. Nobody'd notice that. If you want people *to* notice, send two burly men in white shirts and leather jackets, driving a brown car with no hubcaps, below speed limit, in a residential neighbourhood. They could pretend to be Mormons, except Mormons wear ties and carry Bibles, they don't drive right up to your house and nobody else's, they're not over fifty with bellies out over their belts, and they don't check all up and down the street while they wait for you to answer the doorbell. Neither do the Jehovah Witnesses, but they leave my house a helluva lot faster than these guys did.

Anyway, they came in and meeted and greeted a bit and then they asked me if I'd be up for a little special assignment from time to time.

You know I would, I told them, I sure as hell would. Depending, of course.

It wouldn't be steady, they said, and it wouldn't be exactly official. But it would be good work.

Meaning that I'd like the work or that I'd like the pay?

Both, they said. Both.

So I slid the franchise kit into the side pocket of my La-Z-Boy and pulled the stick-shift that hikes up the footrest. I love that chair.

Spill, I said.

They confessed that from time to time they have a suspect that they know is guilty as sin, but they haven't got the goods on him, and can't get the wily bastard to give them the clues they know he has.

Well, I knew that much. That's why I did what I did that time, but that's over now. At least they kept me out of the local facility. I'd be toast in there. Burnt toast. Shredded wheat. The breakfast of champions. I put too many people in there myself.

Now, there are only so many legal ways of inter-rogating a suspect, what with lawyers and rights and all that. Don't get me wrong, I'm all for people's rights and fairness and decency. That's why I'm in the business. But some people just plain give up their rights, as far as this citizen is concerned, when they sell drugs to kids, or steal from little local corner stores or rape women or children or murder hard-working people like cabbies or their own fam-ily. No rights for them. Pond scum has more rights. I'd be way kinder to pond scum than I'd be to these low-lifes if I was left alone for an evening's entertain-ment with one of them.

I didn't think these enforcers of Halifax's laws would let me exercise my preferred kind of interrogation techniques, and I was right. There'd always be witnesses, they said. Possibly lawyers, though I could open the window to keep the air fresh if there were. That's a joke.

Anyway, there'd be cops to keep the suspect in hand, meaning I was to keep my hands off him or her, and maybe lawyers, and recordings, and no rough stuff, blah, blah, blah. But they wanted me to interrogate certain special cases.

Well, I had to ask why. They've got lots of Inspectors on staff. What'd they want me to do that they couldn't do on their salary?

Here's what floored me: they actually came right out and said that I was the best interrogator they knew and they didn't know how I did it, I just did it, and I could do it just as well without the violence. If there was a weak link in a suspect's armour, I could find it, and get him to confess just like I was Billy Graham asking him if he loved Jesus.

Which is true. I just know where to lean sometimes, where the soft spots are, and I couldn't tell you most of the time how I know. Hunches, I guess.

Heck, if you really want to know, I'm chasing bad clues most of the time, but I just keep at it until I uncover the one clue that's good. What else would you do? I've hunted down more false leads, wild geese, garden paths, pipe dreams, dead ends, you name it. The thing about being a good PI is you just have to go and check out absolutely everything. Everything. The crazy stuff and the normal stuff. And pay attention. That's key.

Now, being off the street, as it were, I wasn't so sure. How could I interview a suspect based on some staff gumshoe's hack work? If the evidence went running around in pumps and peacock feathers singing a Barry Manilow song after five o'clock, some of those career guys'd never find it. I suppose that's how they get to make it a career. Bullets fly after dark, but if you're home for supper every night, they won't find you. Keeps the wives and kids happy. You get to collect a pension that way, retire with a fishing rod in a little speedboat out on Grand Lake. Can't blame them for wanting that. But I didn't think I could pick up where they left off and actually be able to nail anything down.

So I said no.

Well, do you know what those big bastards did then? I shouldn't call them that. They're decent guys, really. And gals. I actually like some of them. Anyway, what they did next nearly floored me, literally, and that wasn't easy since I was pretty well buried in my big chair at the time. But I pushed the lever forward and jumped straight up outta that chair when they quietly told me that they knew all about certain activities of mine which they didn't want to tell me they knew, 'cause if it became known that they knew what they knew, they would have to pursue action regarding said activities, which they would prefer not to do at all, as they unofficially had no problem with it.

But they would have a fiduciary responsibility— they actually said that, a *fiduciary responsibility* to act on their knowledge unless they could demonstrate a *quid pro quo*, meaning that they would really like me to agree to try interviewing for them.

I said I didn't know that cops knew any Latin, let alone how to use it properly all in one sentence. I said that just to give myself a moment to think, not to insult them, and they weren't insulted. They're good guys, really. They just sat there and looked at me, placid as bulls in a green field, looking just a little sad as they always do.

They had me, I could see that. The clincher was that I knew they didn't know what they had on me, just that there was something to be found if they looked. And I didn't want them looking.

So I said yes.

~

They had this room all set up in this old office building downtown, not at the station. They would bring a person of interest to this place for quote an interview close quote, before they went to the station for questioning. Off the record if nothing came of it, on the record if a confession or a clue resulted.

So, about this case. You probably remember it, it was in the news for a long time. This lady'd disappeared in the fall, a young mother of a baby, gone missing. I wanted to check it out, but couldn't because of you-know, so I was sitting on my hands when they called me. They'd found her body a couple days earlier. Murdered, natch. They had a suspect, and would I check him out before they took him along to the station for official questioning?

I drove downtown so fast I got there before them, I was that eager.

I walked right past the door to the place twice before I found it. Something about it makes it hard to find, even when you're right there. It's a great location for our business, I'll give them that. If anyone wanted to go back later to—ahem—dispute the procedures, they'd likely give up looking for it.

So they take me up in the rickety old elevator to this office—it's even got pebbled glass in the door just like in those old black and white detective movies—and they show me the reports and photos and et cetera.

Not pretty.

She'd been missing for, what, three or four months, something like that, and while she'd been frozen under snow in the winter, she'd thawed out long before they discovered her. You know, those cops and detectives do have it tough some days. And the family, who have to identify what's left of the remains, if they can. And the medical people have to poke all through everything for evidence and do the autopsy. I've seen my share of that, too. More than I want to. It's hard to forget, once you've seen some things. Very hard.

Anyway.

How they could find evidence in all that decomposed...in those conditions was beyond me, and I wasn't far off the mark: they had basically none, no fingerprints or DNA, anyway. You couldn't find a knife or bullet wound in the...in what was left. So they wanted me to get their prime suspect to just confess. As if.

Well, okay, I said, let's get going. Tell me who you got.

Her husband, they told me.

The grieving, devoted, widowed-father-of-their-little-months-old-baby husband? *That* husband? I nearly slugged them.

I'd seen the guy on the suppertime news and, like everyone else, I suspected him all along. His eyes were all red-rimmed at the funeral, though; he tried to speak and had to give it up like all the best play-actors.

My Spidey-sense had tingled then, but I assumed they would just wait for him to make a mistake to corroborate some piece of evidence. It's not unusual that a man will kill his wife. He might've committed a hundred other justifiable homicides, but he shouldn't've done this one, not to his lovely, young, frankly bodalicious wife.

And now I got to be his first interrogator, without conclusive evidence and with witnesses present. Great.

Another cop brought him up, all apologetic and deferential with him, and so was I. We shook hands and I asked him to sit. The cops sat against the wall in their chairs. No lawyer. He wasn't accused of any-thing. Just brought to me for information purposes, they said, to see if he could help us in our search.

They told him I could help people remember things they didn't know they knew.

Well, where to start?

I told him how sorry I was for his troubles, and he said thank you, and I asked him to tell me what he knew of what had happened, and he told me exactly what I'd seen in the newspapers, nothing more.

Which got my attention, because that was exactly what the official release had been. Not his story, or his take on the story. He told the story exactly as the cops'd asked the reporter to print it in the *Chronicle*.

You know, when they stick a microphone in front of the people on the street in what passes for award-winning journalism we get on TV, people always have an opinion. Always. Even when they don't have a clue what they're talking about, which is most of the time. But opinions are always swarming as thick as black-flies in spring.

So I asked him his opinion of what happened.

Now, our man on the street would have launched into any of a dozen different streams of consciousness, laying the blame somewhere between the government and God. God bless those editors or producers or whoever has to cut out all but the least-worst babble for broadcast. But you know there'd be babble to cut.

Not this guy. Our supposed grieving father and bereaved husband asks me, hostile-like, what did I want, his opinion about *how* his wife was killed or *that* she was found or *how* she was found, or *what*?

See how it gets easy? He's being careful about

where he goes in our little chat. *Ding-ding-ding.* Little bells jingle in my head, and I can see that the waiting bulls have heard them, too. They haven't moved a muscle, but their gaze moved from their shoes to about three feet ahead of them on the floor. They're listening.

See, a non-guilty person doesn't need to be careful of what he says, unless, of course, he is afraid of being falsely accused, which might worry some people. But most innocent folk don't give that a thought. People who're where they shouldn't be when something bad goes down might well be concerned, like being a witness to a crime, or just being up to no good doing something that's not related to the matter at hand. But this guy was supposedly home with his little baby while his wife was gone shopping or something—reasonable alibi but a baby's not a credible witness.

He and his lady were known as a hot couple in their circle. Both were working in good jobs, reasonable assets and reasonable debt—motivation zero. Or unknown, anyway.

Opportunity? Well, that's tied up with alibi.

I asked him what might've been used to kill her. That wasn't in the paper. Sure enough, he didn't know.

But what do you *think* it was? I asked.

Don't *they* know that? he said. Wouldn't it be *obvious* from the *examinations* they did?

Like I'm a doofus. I love it when they think I'm stupid.

It would be if the weapon left a mark, sir, I said, or if there even was a weapon. I'm sure they do know, the medical people, but I haven't got that information yet. I was just wondering what your opinion'd be about that, I said.

Notice I didn't ask him if he *knew* what killed her. That would've been an accusation, ever so slightly, and I didn't want to go there yet.

He didn't know, couldn't say, had no idea.

I apologized for asking, and then asked him how long—in his opinion—how long it would've taken for his wife to die? Just a guess.

He was perspiring just a teeny bit. The newspaper printed that she maybe died of hypothermia if she was unconscious from her wounds and not dead when she was dumped. Knowing how she was killed would be insider information that only forensics or the murderer would have. Thin ice to speculate on.

I don't know, he said.

Couldn't you guess? I asked.

Oh, quickly, I suppose, he said, just like that, blasé as anything. *Oh, quickly, I suppose.*

Now, if you were this guy, what would you be thinking about right at this point? You'd be thinking about what you did—if you're the guilty party—and how you can't tell the truth but instead you have to tell another story, and you'd also be thinking about me and what I know and what I'm going to ask you next. That's a lot to think about. Things can go wrong.

Did she die where she was found, do you think? I

asked him.

Again, you could see him mentally reviewing the newspaper story.

It's possible, he said carefully.

I asked him why he'd say that.

I don't know, he says, kinda loud. You asked me to guess, so I guessed.

Well, could it have happened another way? I asked, and he said he supposed so.

Now he sees we're moving attention from the body itself to where the crime was committed. If we move we could jump anywhere. That's scary, if you did it.

Do you and your wife like to make meals together? I asked. I'm sorry, I meant, *did* you?

He told me he didn't think that was relevant.

The bulls looked right up at him.

I thought I'd just play my best card then without any more build-up and see what happened. He was a school teacher, taught chemistry. I knew that from the news stories, but I asked him anyway what he did for a living.

You know what I do, he said. He's as defensive as all hell now. Jingle all the way.

That's when the sore throat hit me.

I'm asking him if he ever brought chemicals home from school, maybe experimented with them in his kitchen, when I felt my ears shut off and huge pressure building inside my head.

He said of course not, but I could hardly hear him, so I begged his pardon, and he said it louder. Quite a bit louder.

As I'm getting to my zinger question, the hot wire wrapped around my throat. So when I asked him if he poisoned his wife at home and then dumped her in the woods where she died an excruciating death from chemical burns from the inside out, which was all guess-work on my part, it hurt so much to speak that my eyes watered and my voice went all funny so it sounded like I was all torn up with emotion.

The cops were looking at me then, all concerned to see me taking it so hard, and the perp was surprised because he had been expecting a lot more Q&A, and now he's thrown right off base.

You see, the guilty prepare for suspicion from one direction, and they can defend pretty hard when they know where it's coming from. So he was prepared to keep batting my questions back like we're playing ping-pong, which is often how it goes. Which drives me crazy. Which is why I sometimes used to use a little physical intervention, just to break the monotony for us both.

So here I was, croaking out my big question, which basically told him we know how his wife was killed and we knew he did it, and then I couldn't hardly talk. My big moment in my new job for the cops and I'm wimping out.

I was feeling very loopy all of a sudden. My ears were plugged solid. My throat was on fire and it hurt like hell to swallow, and when I did my eyes leaked. I have to tell you, I'm a sook when it comes to being sick. I just wanted to be home in my La-Z-Boy with a rum toddy and a snuggly blanket, to tell you the God's-honest truth. This non-physical interrogation was taking too long.

I was reeling like I was hit from behind, and then I heard voices through the guck in my ears.

I looked up, and there he was, appealing to the big cops, saying he didn't have to put up with this shit, he'd never been so insulted in his life, he knew people high up downtown and all that.

You know, those of us in the investigations profession, if I can call it that, when we hear the chorus, we know we're going to hear the whole song sooner or later, know what I mean? They're more innocent than ten saints, they'll make us pay, we'll hear from their lawyers, they're friends with the Mayor or their MP, all that stuff comes out in a real loud voice. I should get it put to music so they could sing it.

The cops told him to please keep it down, sir. That's all they had to say, and he did it. They looked back at me, so he looked at me, too. I looked at them and wondered how I could carry on. Because you can't call in sick on this beat.

The big envelope the cops gave me with all the pictures and reports in it was on the desk. I reached in the envelope and took out a picture. I have no idea what it was of, because my vision was all blurry with the plague that was creeping up the back of my throat toward my brain, but I managed to ask him in a whisper if he wanted to see it. I drooled from the pain of saying that much, and I wiped my mouth with my sleeve. I suppose I looked a little bit crazy, I don't know.

But he declined to look at the picture. So I looked at it. And then I took out another one and pretended to look at *it* for a while. And another and another, until I had them all out on the desk, face up, facing him. If he wanted not to see what was in them he'd have to look at the ceiling.

Then I said to him, just mouthing the words above a whisper, that I thought she likely lived for a couple hours after he dumped her before she finally succumbed, and that it was a mercy it was cold that night or else she would have suffered a lot longer. But the pain of her final hours would have been beyond describing, because an apparent blow to her head hadn't killed her. I told him if her voice-box hadn't been burned with whatever he had made her drink, someone might have heard her call for help from the shallow grave he had dug for her, but it was a mercy that she died, in the end, after what he did to her.

Then I was truly done. Done in. Maybe I was feeling, I dunno, what do the shrinks call it, psycho-somatic, like what she'd felt, but I know I never had such a sore throat in all my life before or since, knock on wood, and I just couldn't speak another word. I just sat there, dabbing at my eyes, wiping my spit when I waited too long to swallow, probably moaning a bit when I thought my eardrums would burst under the pressure.

The big cops just sat there, looking mournful but alert. They knew enough not to interfere without a signal from me. That poor woman's murderous husband was just sitting there, too. If I wasn't so preoccupied with how bad I was feeling I would've loved to pop him one.

The cops described to me later how he changed. He'd been yelling that he was unjustly accused, as I said. Then he crossed his arms over his chest and looked very cool and superior while I was studying the pictures of his dead wife's corpse, the bastard. He couldn't decide whether to look interested or disinterested or something in between when I was telling him about her horrible death. I would've given him more details too, organ by organ, if I could've spoken more. The cops said he just seemed to lose his grip on his act. Since I'd stopped talking, according to those ping-pong rules of engagement it was his turn to speak, and he just couldn't find his way to the right words.

The pressure was coming at him from a different direction now, see, and he was off-kilter. Hadn't prepared a good act for this because he never expected us to catch on.

Isn't that a caution? Everyone always suspects the husband, but the husbands always believe that they'll be considered innocent forever because they're such great actors and have concocted such a great story. He never expected us to find her body in the woods anyway, at least not until it had totally rotted from whatever he had poured down her throat and over her body.

But like I tell all the perps, you can pick the loneliest, unlikeliest place in the province to hide your evidence, but the next day some family will come zooming right by in their four-wheel ATV and see your tracks, or their stupid dog will chase a rabbit into the woods and then start digging up what you've just buried and carry a piece home. If you got there, so can we. So don't get comfy, because we're coming to get you, and the TV cameras will follow right behind us, that's what I tell them.

I hope they all have nightmares about me. We'd be even.

I don't know how long it was after that, I was pretty woozy, but he started breathing funny, and as bad as I felt, he looked worse. Sweat was running down his face. We probably looked like the Bobbsey Twins at the Spa, sweating and looking miserable at each other.

He asked if he could smoke.

No he couldn't, the cops said.

Then he asked them if he could use the washroom.

No he couldn't, they answered him together without missing a beat, like Bobbsey Triplets themselves. These guys crack me up sometimes, they really do.

Not to pee, he said. Throw up.

You wouldn't think that men that big could move that fast. One got the waste can under his chin and another pushed his head into it fast. When they let him up, he brought out an embroidered cotton handkerchief from his pocket to wipe his mouth and

I remember thinking that his wife probably bought it for him for a romantic gift. What a gormless shit he was.

I gotta say, I really don't get these people. What goes so wrong, why does it seem so bad, that murder is the best idea they can come up with, especially in such a sadistic way as he did to this lovely young woman?

Know what I think? I think, when they have these big school graduations, they should forget about getting speakers to tell the students to aim high and be true to themselves and all that folderol. Most people try to do that anyway, in their way. They will or they won't. The progress of society isn't affected by what convocation speakers say.

They should just turn up the lights in the auditorium and tell the students to look around them, because in spite of all the time and money they've borrowed and spent to get a university degree, one or two of them will decide in their pathetic lifetimes that the best way to overcome some minor mouse-turd of adversity is to kill someone they work with or—think of the brilliance—someone they love or who loves them, more's the pity. And if that should happen, they should know that they've proved they're terminally stupid pieces of crap, no matter what degree they've just been given. Just *idiot*, no *savant*.

The TV reporters always, *always* say they're waiting to learn a murderer's motive, and people watch the late news to see it like if the Hubble telescope discovered a used Kleenex on Mars. As if we care. Motive may help us to catch a killer, but once he's caught, who gives a shit about his motive?

Why did I kill her, M'Lud? Oh, because I'm an idiot, sire, too effing stupid to think of anything better to do, like offing myself instead and doing the world a favour.

Motivation, bullshit.

I guess now you know how I really feel about that.

Anyway, baby-face there was whimpering into his monogrammed hanky, and then he started to cry. He boo-hooed like a girl, and retched, bending over and swaying and saying things I couldn't catch and generally carrying on like a man possessed, which I suppose he was at that point.

When he held his breath to blow his nose, I leaned over and croaked that if he'd confess we wouldn't make him go over all the details any more, which wasn't exactly true, but truth is very plastic in these situations.

He nodded and then he hiccuped I-did-it and I thought we had him, but one of the cops said that wouldn't be good enough. Our boy got a look of horror on his face, but I knew what the cop meant.

I pantomimed to the murdering creep that he had to say out loud that he killed his wife by administering poison to her, which we needed him to do for the audio record that had been running since we brought him into the room.

He took a deep breath and announced it right out loud then, just like he was on the radio.

We were done.

The cops produced enough hardware from their belts and jackets then to restrain a riot. Normally I would've been one of the people needing restraint once I got a confession, but I was so far gone by then —I never thought it could happen, even after a good fight—that instead of holding me back the cops had to hold me up and pretty much carry me out of there.

They drove me straight to the ER, where I'm ashamed to say I got seen ahead of a lot of sick people in the waiting room, but I was grateful for that, and for the antibiotic IV, too. The boys in blue came by the hospital for me the next morning and drove me home, as sweet as anything.

It was a couple of days before I recovered enough to remember that my car was still parked somewhere downtown off Barrington Street. I called the cops about it and they laughed and laughed on the phone, which annoyed me a bit.

Then they told me to haul my ass out of my La-Z-Boy and look in my driveway.

My car was there, with a fistful of tickets tucked under the wiper, along with a bill for the tow and impounding charge.

All stamped *Paid in Full.*

Jan Fancy Hull

Suite 102: The Wordist

Good evening Your Honour, esteemed head table, fellow honoured guests, members of the Greater Halifax Wholistic Arts Society, ladies and gentlemen. Thank you for inviting me to speak at your annual dinner. As you know, I am filling in at the last minute for your originally-advertised and prominent guest speaker, a nationally-known and published author, who has been unavoidably detained. My name is not nearly so well-known, but I shall attempt to be entertaining, if less acerbic, nonetheless.

Thanks also for your kind, if short, introduction, Madam Chair. It could be longer only if there were more to say about me than that I am an aspiring author. Aspiring to be published, that is. However, I persevere. I write.

Now, to earn the stipend you offered, I speak to you on Aspects of Writing.

Firstly, I call myself a wordist, rather than a writer. Writing is the grand process, but words are the raw material, and I like to be mindful that I imagine stories out of words, these mysterious little entities, like atoms, that carry so much meaning or so little meaning or such great potential for meaning, or act as hinges or nails for the Main Thought. Letters of the alphabet would be the molecules in those atoms.

In the same vein as wordist, a creator of paintings should call himself a paintist, or one who carves stones, a stoneist, in my opinion, to pay homage to the medium one uses in the creations. A musician calls himself a flutist or accordionist to ascribe a little credit to the instrument with which he makes the music—if an accordion's noises are considered music.

A composer of music should call himself a pitchist or noteist. No, ma'am, a pitchist. *Pitch*-ist. The composer has a finite number of pitches to arrange on the page, yet they are so versatile, so obliging, so malleable and ductile. If you use the well-tempered concert piano as a guide, there are only eighty-eight notes with which to create Wagner's *Ring Cycle*, and that's pretty amazing, though it necessitates a lot of duplication and repetition.

To write, I select from the five thousand or so words in common use in our language plus a few from other languages, living and dead, and I also have to know what a lot of them mean. But pity help me if, finding a good word, in my delight with it I dare to repeat it in a story. Critics and editors pounce on and denounce such things.

Music in Bach's day had rules, but nowadays you can use any of the eighty-eight notes in any order, for any duration. It's not all bad. Modern composers write some of the most mesmerizing and mystical music using very few of those notes.

There's nothing available like that to a wordist. If I wrote "Tell me true, tell me, do: Do you love me, love me, too?" over and over and over, would you read it? Would you recommend my book to your friends? No, you wouldn't. But a minimalist composer could write the musical equivalent of it and the critics would hoist him on their shoulders. It isn't fair.

If music puts you to sleep, you love it. Ravel's *Bolero* comes to mind, or things by Brahms. If a book puts you to sleep, you hate it. Wordists have a hard time coming to terms with this. We often wish we had kept up with our piano lessons, which seem simpler in retrospect.

What I write with my words is stories. Or should I say *are* stories? Grammar is such a pain in my arsenal, yet without it I'm lost. I'm not myself a grammarian, but I confess there is one in my family. They are so unbending and unrepentant about its rules. Zealots, even. Some are quite aggressive.

I like to write language as she is spoke in the mouths of my characters. So many people today speak what I call *languish*, grammatically and idiomatically incorrect language. And I don't just mean teenagers or those for whom English is not their mother tongue, or if it is, their mothers spoke it with a free hand. Just listen to yourselves, there, at your tables. All around you are incomplete sentences, half-baked thoughts, runny pronunciations, starts and stops, subjects and verbs disagreeing so vigorously that you might wonder if there is not some physical or psychical damage going on that science hasn't detected yet. One day we may discover that errors in grammar contribute to brain lesions, or gastric reflux, or irritable bowel syndrome, or poor results on the stock market. Further study is warranted, I suggest.

But wordists must respect grammar, because if you don't know the rule about participles, say, you don't know how to dangle 'em to good effect. There's a difference between being funny and being annoying. That's what you tell your children. Most wordists are like children; musicians are, too. Inadvertent mistakes in grammar are like the wrong notes in music. If music still accepts that there is such a thing as a wrong note, that is.

But, back to me. One thing I will tell you about myself as a wordist is that I am always at dead ends or loose ends.

In the dead end category, what I can write about with any authority is quite limited. Because of the length of time I spent achieving my extensive education, I personally have no field of expertise, natural or acquired.

But many of my characters know a great deal about many things. My characters rescue me

Most of the characters I create are composites of many people I have met or wished I had or hadn't. But if you think that real people—singers or bike shop owners or singing bike shop owners—act like lemmings or birds in a flock or fish in a school, you are sadly misinformed. One cannot predict the behaviour of 'people' of any type or genus when taken in units of one. Even pollsters admit a margin of error that is at least twenty people wide, nineteen times out of twenty.

This is a good thing. There have been about half a million detective stories written, and they're all different in some way, because each character makes choices in what to say or do in every chapter, every page, every paragraph, every sentence, and, yes, every word. No stories need be exactly alike, although stereotypes do tend to slither in if we rush, or write in the evenings after the requisite cocktail hour, often our only reward for years on end.

By the way, that was a fib about the half-million detective stories. I have no idea whether that is even remotely accurate or ludicrously erroneous. I have no facts at my beck and call, and rarely go looking for them unless I have had the poor judgment to get my characters embroiled in an argument hinging on some fact or proof I am to supply. Facts are dead ends, and I have plenty of those already.

What my characters need to know, *they* know. What they state as gospel has to work for them, but don't ask me to prove the veracity of their beliefs.

One of my favourite authors, the great Jeanette Winterson, has one of her characters say to the reader, "Trust me. I'm telling you stories." It's brilliantly and transparently manipulative. Just like people.

I once had aspirations to be a journalist. It was the editors' insistence upon facts that turned me from that path. Journalists are not wordists, they are factists. No, sir, not fascists, or not necessarily. *Fact*-ists.

I used 'embroiled' back there. It is actually redundant as I used it. Embroiled means 'in an argument', so to say 'embroiled in an argument' means to be 'in an argument in an argument'. There is nothing like that in music, because music's few rules are so lax. Beethoven wrote measure upon measure of redundant music, Mozart went overboard with it, yet we revere them. Poets are similarly carried away, but their words are often put to music so they are aiders and abettors rather than exceptions to the rule.

As you can see, defining words is akin to splitting atoms, or hairs. Split hairs are not nearly as explosive, but they are famously aggravating. Not to mention split infinitives, and I'd rather not. Sometimes it is just better to write the darn words than to shave them too closely. We are not doing nuclear fission here, nor making soup. We are simply telling you stories.

You can trust story-tellers more than you can the factists. Think about it. Like a stopped watch, fiction may be true twice a day, while some facts are false all day long.

To be fair, if you split notes in a musical performance, it is considered a bad thing unless it's jazz, which is all about notes that are split until they bleed blue, which leads to all sorts of trouble, and that is why mothers don't want their babies growing up to be jazz singers. First the notes bend and slide, and then...

I struggle with ambiguity, and with similes. Also,

you may be thinking, with absurdity, but that comes with the story-teller's territory. Life is often absurd, but is it plausible?

You might be waiting to hear how I research my characters, but I do no research other than to observe life around me. I find material everywhere. To illustrate, I will describe the people who shared the little office building where I used to write, who may someday become characters in my stories.

Excuse me. Pardon? Oh, I see. The kitchen asks for your indulgence as the *crème brulées* have caught fire, so I have a little extra time before dessert is served. Imagine our good fortune.

For some years, I kept a writing studio in a small office in a building wedged between more attractive features on Barrington Street. The entrance was obscure, set back from the sidewalk and not inviting to walk-in traffic, which is just how I wanted it. You see, I am a vocal writer. That is to say, I speak the dialogue out loud to hear it, to see if it sounds authentic.

One of my characters—and by the way, in fiction it's all characters; non-fiction has people—one of my characters might be accused of a nasty crime of which he will claim to be innocent. How will he state his claim, with what words, and in what order? Shall he say "I'm innocent!"? That hardly seems credible; too cliché. "I'm not guilty"? Too stilted for most crooks. "I didn't do it!"? Better. "I'm offended and I got rights and I'm friends with the Mayor and you're gonna hear from him!"? I like that best. Maybe I'll have the guilty party shout all those phrases. It's messy and stupid, and don't you find that's what life is really like? It is if you're a crook. Or me, too, much of the time. Not that I'm a crook, but I think like one when I am writing about crooks.

Anyway, in order to test these nuances of dialogue, I find myself speaking them out loud, which can sound a bit odd if you're on the other side of my studio door. Whenever I am deep in dialogue it seems someone is within earshot, in spite of my having sought out this office for its solitude.

So that's how I met my fellow tenants and character models: a vendor of dreams, a painter, a minister, a private eye—oh, excuse me, what are those bells? A fire alarm? No, really? But I'm not—yes, of course, we must evacuate. It's probably just the burnt sugar in the kitchen, but we mustn't take chances.

Please, come back as soon as we receive the all-clear. You mustn't miss the remainder of your evening: your dessert, for which you've paid, and the rest of my story, for which you haven't. Good value, both. Please rise now and remain in your place until Her Honour and the Head Table have left the room, then everyone take the nearest exit.

Thank you.

(To be continued.)

Suite 103: The Dreams Broker

YOUR DREAMS MADE POSSIBLE
Appt not req.
Ste103 - 1950 Barrington

"Good afternoon. May I help you?"

"Oh, hi. Am I in the right place? I mean, it's not the easiest place to find, is it? And there's no parking for blocks."

"You are looking for…?"

"Oh, sorry, I came about the ad? In the paper? Dreams For Sale?"

"Not for sale. Made possible. Yes, you are in the right place. *Entrez, s'il vous plaît.* Be seated. My name is Claire Spiegel. You are?"

"Uh, Brian."

"Welcome, Brian. You have a dream."

"No, well, maybe, but I was wondering, do you have any, well, a brochure or something? Maybe a price-list? I'm not sure why I'm here, and I'm not going to buy anything today, you know? Could you just explain to me how this—how it works?"

"There's no brochure. No price-list."

"Why not?"

"I have nothing to sell."

"Well, what the heck is this, then? What about the ad? I thought I'd check it out, maybe find out how much it would cost to do—to accomplish a dream or something. If your price isn't too high, I mean. I don't have a lot of money for this. Maybe none at all."

"Of course. At first, the price for your dream may seem very high. There are variables, not very many, but they are important. We'll discuss them, and the decision is always yours. I assure you, you have no obligation to me, not now, not ever. We agree to proceed, or we stop. Does that sound acceptable?"

"Yes, m-maybe. We'll see. I don't even know what sort of things you have to sell—to offer. What am I doing here?"

"I will ask you the questions and you will give your honest answers to us both. Ready?"

"Sure, okay, I guess. Shoot."

"'Okay', you 'guess'. 'We'll see'. What do you know for sure, Brian? On your way here, while you were searching for a downtown parking space, what was in your mind? What brought you here? Why did you come?"

"Well, I was hoping you'd have a list of things I could choose from to do—to accomplish. You know, tasks or assignments. Important challenges, right? That sounds weird, but that's what I dream about."

"You dream of doing something important?"

"Yeah, like—I know this sounds crazy, but like, oh,

I don't know, like rescuing a damsel in distress—that sounds cheesy—or smuggling something important across a border, like in the movies...for the good guys, of course, not something stupid like a drug mule. I know you can't make that happen, but I thought you might have something for me to do. Maybe like real-time role-play."

"Role-play?"

"Yeah, you know, like pretending, like those paint-ball shoot-outs where you get to kill all your co-workers but it's just for fun."

"Killing your co-workers is fun?"

"No, no, not for real, no! I was just saying that as an example. Okay, bad example. Look, in my job—I'm a salesman—we practise different situations we might encounter with clients so we'll know what to say when it comes up for real. We call it role-play. I thought you might have some kind of role for me to play that would give me a sense of...oh forget it. There's nothing like that for me here, is there...or anywhere."

"Of course there is. Not here, specifically, but in your future there certainly is a great role for you to play. We have some work to do, of course, but you do not mind a little work, do you, Brian?"

"Gosh, no. I love to work. I can work hard. This job I have now is easy, well, sort of, but I'm not very good at it yet...I know that doesn't make sense, but anyway, I can find time to do some other work. As long as my boss doesn't find out - if it's on company time."

"Good. Your boss need not know anything of this. So, congratulations! You are on your quest already."

"Hardly. What've I done?"

"You would not believe how many people are not able to say what you have just said—that you are willing to work to see your dream become possible. Your challenge, or one of them, is that your dream is still indistinct, and that makes it harder to get there. Not impossible, never impossible, but a few steps extra. I have every confidence that we will find it. Now, how much will you pay?"

"For what?"

"To have your dream become possible."

"I was asking *you* that. How much does it cost? This is a crazy business, Miss. You have nothing to sell, and now you're asking me how much it costs."

"No, I am not asking you how much anything costs. I asked you how much you will pay. There is a very big difference. I am not selling shoes, nor are you bartering for used goods at the flea market. I am asking you to think very hard now, Brian. Think about where you go in your head all the time, before you go to work, between sales calls, on weekends, when you were searching in the newspaper classifieds and found my advertisement. What were you dreaming of, and how much would you pay to make that dream possible?"

"Okay. You got me now. I know from our sales training that whoever speaks first after that question loses, so I guess I've lost now, no offence. I guess I could afford about fifty. A month, I mean. I'm trying to save up, too, you know, for a house. That's a dream, too, but I know how that one comes true—lots and lots of moolah."

"Ah, yes. I see. I also see our time is up. Until next week, then. Bring your fifty when you return. And Brian, keep in mind: you will have work to do."

~

"Look. I can go to Lose-to-Win or NewMe or any of those established hucksters and pay a lot less than that—and some of them even include food, such as it is. Even Waist Watchers charges less than twenty a week, but you have to do all your own cooking, which is not my skill. I've tried 'em all and I never heard of a weight-loss plan that cost five hundred dollars a week—and no food included, no surgical procedure, not even pills or a machine to make you jiggle it off! Christ, lady, at that price, I won't even be able to afford my own food!"

"Precisely, Edward. Shall we continue?"

"But I have to eat. Everybody eats. I need money for groceries, and for my wife's credit card. You said you could make my dream of being a normal weight possible. What you are proposing instead is robbery!"

"If you define robbery as taking money from you against your will and leaving nothing in return, it would be. But you will give me your money willingly and receive something in return that you value more. At the least, better I should rob you than you should rob yourself, *n'est-ce pas*? That way, you can see that it is happening. When we rob from ourselves, it is so hard to see. We train ourselves not to see it, more accurately. You may not understand this at this moment, but you will. The simple question you face is this, Edward: who should have that money, you or me? You may keep it and carry on as before with this and that diet, paying less and getting less, but that is what has brought you to me. Or you can pay five hundred dollars each week to me and your dream of being a normal weight will immediately become possible. You choose. One way can work; the other has not."

"Well, for how long, then? How long do I have to pay you this—this extortion money before I see results? And what precisely will you be doing in return?"

"It is not extortion. You know that. Careless language will not help you now. It is what you will pay willingly to make your dream become possible. How long until you see results? I daresay you will experience significant changes the moment you leave here. As for what I will do: I will not do or deny myself anything that will in any way affect your dream of *you* being of normal weight. You will continue to pay me as long as you choose to come here. And I remind you that we can terminate our arrangement at any time. No contract, no refunds. No obligation to continue."

"Oh, what the hell. No. I'll come back next week and I'll...I'll let you know then, if I do."

"Perhaps you will, but it is unlikely. If you do, the payment will be higher, success more remote. I recommend you start now before indecision steals your money from both of us."

"This is entirely confidential?

"If you keep it so."

"Fine, then. Well, it's not fine, but I don't know what else to do. You'll take a cheque, I assume?"

"Yes, that is acceptable. *Merçi*, Edward."

"Call me Montcalm, please. Everyone calls me Montcalm, except my wife calls me Monty. Look, don't you have something to guide me—a diet for me to follow? A book? Exercise plan? Pill? Bracelet? Eight-hundred number? Bible verses? Anything?"

"I know you are afraid, Edward. This is to be expected. But fear can also be understood. You are afraid of yourself without a system, of what you might do, of what you have always done, regardless of those so-called aids. But you have just agreed to remove the power – that is, the money - necessary for you to carry on in that fashion. In fact, you have changed the game altogether in this moment. Because of that, your dream is already possible. Come back next week. We must finish now. *A bientôt*."

~

"Hey, Miss. I know you introduced yourself last time but I forgot your name right away. That's bad, because in sales we know that the sweetest sound a customer can hear is his own name—"

"*Bonjour*, Brian. Did you bring your fifty?"

"'Scuse me? Oh, the fifty dollars? Yeah, I did, but I need to ask you what it's for, since you didn't do anything, really, last week."

"May I have it, please?"

"Well, okay, but that's for a month, right?"

"Please sit. My name is Claire, *encore*. Claire Spiegel. Now, tell me about your week."

"Well, I'm in sales, right? And I told you I was finding it hard to get the orders, but, boy-oh-boy, I did something right, 'cause I landed my biggest orders ever! I was Rep of the Week. My boss announced it at our Monday morning meeting, in front of everybody: Brian Smith, Sales Rep of the Week!"

"Congratulations, Brian! I do not have to ask how you feel about that. What do you sell?"

"Oh, well. I wish you hadn't asked. I sell personal paper products. Um, personal hygiene, waste removal...toilet paper, s-sanitary napkins, adult diapers, things like that. I'm a manufacturer's representative. I sell to pharmacies and convenience stores and such."

"And I will not ask how you feel about that, either. It looks painful. Tell me, what do you think about your week?"

"Well, when I left here I really believed that something was gonna change in my life, and I guess I was still feeling that when I made those calls, so I took some chances and got the sales. I'll make bonus, too, which makes it easier to pay you—but don't go getting ideas about raising the price on me. Anyway, I felt pretty good all weekend too. And then Monday, at that meeting, wow! In fact, I felt pretty chuffed until you asked me about my product line just now. Geez. That was a fast drop on the ol' Ferris wheel."

"What happened, do you think?"

"I dunno, I...I guess I think I'm still just a loser who sells ass-wipe, 'scuse my French. Even if I'm good at it, where's the glory in that? How can I go to the pub with my buddies and buy a round for them because I'm the top purveyor of absorbent underwear for seniors? The better I get at my job, the worse my life gets. Can you imagine if I meet a nice girl, I could tell her not to buy tampons 'cause I can get her some manufacturer's samples for free? There's a turn-on. Not."

"Why did you come here?"

"When?"

"This week. Last week. And you brought money this time. Why?"

"Because of your stupid ad! 'Dreams Made Possible'! I dream about...I want to do something great, to feel that I can really accomplish something. Can you do that for me or not?"

"You are already doing that for yourself, Brian. You left here last week and rang the bell at the fairground, so to speak, in one swing of the hammer. Maybe it was not exactly the bell you wanted to ring, but you proved that you can do it. You know you can do that again, every week, and so you shall. But when I told you last week that you had work to do, I was not thinking of your job, as that work was already there for you to do. The real work is learning what damsel you want to rescue, and from what kind of distress. Evidently, though their distress is real, elderly damsels with incontinence problems are not your heart's target, *oui*?"

"Geez, no, I'd have to agree with you there. So where is my damsel, then? How do I find her and rescue her? Boy, wouldn't that make a great story at the pub!"

"Indeed. Where do you live, Brian?"

"Where? Here. In the city, I mean. West end. I live with, I mean, I board, with my—uh, with a family."

"What family?"

"Why?"

"Your parents?"

"Okay, yes, with my parents. But I pay them rent. I told you, Miss, I'm saving to buy a house someday so I can get out of there and, uh, be my own man."

"You must get out now."

"What? Whaddya mean get out—to where? Buy a house? Now? You're crazy. I can't afford that, not yet. Not for a hundred years, maybe sooner if I keep making bonus."

"No, not to buy a house, Brian. To board, if that is what you can afford. Listen carefully to me now. Go find a nice home in the suburbs or beyond and board there. Not with your own family. Go to a community outside the city far enough that they have a volunteer fire department. Do it now. Come back in two weeks. Bring your fifty again. That will be all for now. Good-day."

~

"What are you, here, a fortune-teller? Or a hooker?"

"How may I help you?"

"You heard me, lady. I saw your ad in the classifieds and I was curious. How do you make dreams come true? You can't, you know. That's crap. Dreams are just last night's pizza, or a lumpy pillow. Too bad, though. A big turkey dinner used to keep me really entertained, if you know what I mean. At my age, that's a bonus, to have a great dream like that and still get a good night's sleep. But if you can make the dream come true in the daytime when I'm already awake, well, I'd be really interested in that. How much?"

"How much did you bring?"

"What'll a hundred get me?"

"Your fondest dream."

"Well, hey now, that's great, honey. Let's get started!"

"The money today, and your true dream tomorrow."

"Oh-ho, not so fast, now, sweetie. How do I know you're not going to gyp me?"

"Have you ever had a dream like yours come true before?"

"No, of course not, but—"

"Never?"

"Not since I got married, and that wasn't yesterday."

"And now you are willing to put a hundred dollars

to the test?"

"Your ad said you could do it."

"Then give me your hundred and come back to-morrow. Or go now and never return. Your choice."

"Oh, darn. Can't make it tomorrow, love. Got someone—something else to do. Day after tomorrow good for you?"

"The day after tomorrow will be fine. But you must leave your money with me now."

"Can I—can I have a receipt for it?"

"Of course not. *Merçi. A bientôt.*"

~

"It's not for me, Miss. It's my son. He—he's handicapped, but he tries so hard, and I wish just once he could have a dream come true for him."

"Not come true. Made possible."

"Yeah, well, whatever. I'm a single mom, you see, and his no-good father disappeared once he found out that the baby was going to be Down's. I was on welfare for a long time, but now he's in special day-care so I can work some, and we still have no money, though my family are good to us, it's just not going to make any difference to him, he thinks it's his fault, and it's not, he's such a sweet boy, really, wouldn't harm anyone, but people shun him, you know, or make fun of him, and he says 'It's okay, Mommy' when I get mad at them and I cry, I do, I get depressed, wouldn't you, well, maybe you wouldn't, but you're a smart lady so you wouldn't have got yourself knocked up by the likes of that bastard—oh, sorry, but he was, though I didn't know how bad at the time, about all the drugs and that, but he's probably the reason Kyle is retarded, though the doctor said that was highly unlikely, that's how he said it, too, '*high*-ly un-*like*-ly', looking down his nose at me as if to say he knew who was retarded, but the social worker didn't even care that I taught Kyle to talk pretty good for what he is, she just wanted to put him in a Home, and I know they'd just treat him like a vegetable there, or worse, I've been in those places and I've seen what they do, so no, you're goddamn right I wasn't going to let them take him, and then I saw your ad in the paper and I said to Kyle, 'Look at that, Ky, someone who is putting it right out there that dreams can happen', and you have no idea what a relief it was for me to read that because I'm so tired of being surrounded by negative-thinkers when I myself am a positive-thinker, so—"

"Wait, please. I must catch up and absorb what you have said. Did you tell me what is your dream that you wish to make possible?"

"Oh, I don't want anything for myself, Miss. I gave that up when Ky was born and that no-good deadbeat left us. I knew then there would be no dreams come true for me in this world. I just want to see something good happen for him—for Kyle."

"I see. I am afraid I cannot help you."

"What? Why not? Don't you think he deserves some happiness?"

"Yes, I think your son deserves happiness. Everyone does; it is our fondest wish, though few know what would accomplish it for themselves. But here in my practice, I work only with the person who has a dream she or he wishes to be made possible. You cannot bring someone else's dream to me. If I were to give you a pill, it would not ease some other person's pain, would it? So, I cannot help you. There will be no charge for today. *Au revoir.*"

"But wai—what'll I do? How can I make it better for Kyle? He deserves happiness, he's just a little boy, he doesn't understand..."

"You care deeply about your son, I see. I would not want to see anything less from parents of any child, though I do see much less, too often. You truly want Kyle to have his dream become possible?"

"Yes, oh yes, I really do. I don't know how I can pay you, but I can work overtime, I'll get it somehow, just tell me what I have to do."

"Come back next week, then. Bring Kyle."

"Bring Kyle? But he—he's a—he can't—"

"You must bring him. That is essential. Good-bye now."

~

"Hey, I'm back. Bet you were hoping I'd go away and you could keep the money for nothin', didn't ya?"

"Hello. No, I was hoping you would return. Please come in."

"Funny how you don't give appointments, but I can always get in. Business slow, is it?"

"Business is always as it should be. Please sit down. My name is Claire Spiegel. And you are?"

"I'm Al. Look, uh, I was thinking. Maybe we should just call the whole thing off, you know, what I was talking about the other day…just refund my money and no hard feelings, eh?"

"Yes, I agree, Al, we shall call that whole thing off, no hard feelings. But since you are here, please sit down and tell me a little about yourself. I am about to make some tea. Would you like to join me?"

"Hey, sure, I'd love a cup. Emma—my wife—used to make us tea every afternoon, about this time of day, as a matter of fact…said it restored her. It perked me up too, it really did."

"And where is she now?"

"I wish I knew."

"She's missing?"

"Oh, she's at home, but her mind has gone wandering, and I guess it's not coming back. I'd do anything for her, but it doesn't seem to make any difference. Goddamn old-timer's disease. Why can't they just give you a pill? Her or me, either way's okay with me. She wouldn't miss me now if I was gone…"

"Did you and your wife enjoy being together?"

"Forty-seven years of wedded bliss we had, and still counting, but no more wedded bliss, if you know what I mean."

"I, too, enjoy a cup of tea in the mid-afternoon. But it tastes so much better with good company, does it not? Biscuit?"

"Oh boy, sure. Emma used to give us cookies, too.

She'd natter at me when I dunked them, but I'd do it just to get her going. Can't get her going at all now."

"Al, I wonder, would you be able to assist me here, sometimes?"

"Well, sure, maybe, like what doin'? I'm not as spry as I once was."

"Nothing strenuous. If I need something while I am occupied with a client, I will leave a note for you under the ash-tray in the hallway by the elevator. It would not be anything difficult or expensive, perhaps just to pick up a coffee or two for me or a client, or juice, or a newspaper. Just remember: never knock on my door if it is closed. If there is no note, just leave. Never knock. Could you do that?"

"Why, sure, I could do that, Claire. The home-care ladies come two afternoons a week. They do her toe-nails and hair and stuff like that. Girl-stuff, I call it. Emma doesn't like them to come but I just need to get away sometimes, God forgive me."

"There is nothing to forgive."

"I hope you're right. Well, sure, I could do that for you. Be glad to. It'd be nice to do something for someone who can appreciate it."

"Excellent. If there is no note but my door is open, would you come in and have tea with me some-times?"

"Are you sure you wouldn't mind? That'd be ter-rific. You seem like a very nice lady—a real lady, as a matter of fact. And hey, I'm sorry for, for what I might have said the other day, suggesting you were, well—you know. I was a bit off, I guess, just looking for some—"

"Thank you. I knew that, but it is always good to put right our mis-steps, *n'est-ce pas*? It allows us to return to our better selves. I like your better self, Al, and I look forward to our teas together."

"Are you sure it's okay? People must pay a lot for your services—for whatever it is you do here. I don't want to take up your time..."

"Do not be concerned about that. You have already pre-paid for many cups of tea."

~

"Edward, good morning. *Comment ça va?*"

"I don't know. I really can't say."

"Well, tell me what you can say. Let us review: why did you come to see me?"

"Don't treat me like a child, Miss Spiegel. I came because I read that damn ad in the paper!"

"No, I must contradict you, Edward. Hundreds of people read that 'damn ad', but hundreds do not come here. You did. Why?"

"You know why. Because I want to be a normal size and not have to hump a hundred extra pounds around with me everywhere. And because diets and all that crap don't work for me. And because you said —you *implied*—that you could make it happen for me."

"Good. So you came, and then what?"

"And then you made me five hundred dollars lighter around the wallet, just like snap."

"And then?"

"And then I went home and thought long and hard about how I was going to free up that kind of money to pay you, per week, God help me. I may look successful—and I am—but I'm pretty much tapped out, you know, leveraged. I owe everything I make. Then I thought I must be slipping. That I, Edward K. Montcalm the Second had fallen for a simple con artist. Me, an acknowledged leader in this city's financial community, son of fabled Edward King Montcalm Senior, a lean, mean old bastard who suffered no fools and who founded one of this country's most successful investment firms and countless businesses and buildings and governments. Oh, I ranted and I roared, I assure you. I have a well-stocked bar, and I leaned on it many times for fuel for my ranting. My wife was terrified. My blood pressure would have popped my top if it weren't for those horrid little pills."

"Sounds dramatic. But you are here again."

"Because I don't throw my money away! Even my children have to work a lot harder than you did to get five hundred dollars from me! I preach that you have to follow the dollar to ensure that your investment is a good one. So I'm following my five hundred dollars."

"I must contradict you again, Edward. You are here because you have a dream that you want to make possible. Just because you spend money on something and then follow it does not keep it wise, nor can you make it wise if it is foolish to begin with.

It is your dream you must follow, not the money you pay for it. Never lose sight of your dream, Edward, by calling it something else, something more acceptable to you in your business language. Your road will be hard. There will be setbacks. That is why it is still a dream, do you see, and not your reality already. For some, it is natural to be of normal weight. For you, it is difficult. The price of attaining your valued dream will be very high. You will ask yourself many times, 'Why am I doing this?' Write down the answer if you have to. Have it engraved on the back of one of your watches or on your cuff links. But have it with you, in front of you, all the time. You do not back away from business deals because they are costly or difficult, do you?"

"I most certainly do not."

"Well, this is business of another sort, and it requires something you may not have used much in the past: complete self-honesty. Do you see why? You cannot lie, because you know the lies. You can see through yourself, as it were, because there is no program or gimmick or surgery to hide behind or blame. You cannot cheat, because you will know you are doing it. You must do the difficult thing. Full stop. No secretary, no economy or government or partners or stock market or any of that is involved in this deal. This is you with you. It is personal. It is serious. The good news? What you will learn in this will serve you in all your dealings for the rest of your career. Do you follow?"

"Mostly."

"Did you bring your cheque-book?"

"No."

"Then I mus—"

"Ha! I'm ahead of you on this one, Miss Spiegel. I figured if I came in the door I'd be paying before I left. So, I prepared a cheque and I'll pay you, not because I understand why, but because I'm not ready to stop yet."

"*Bon*. And Edward, in light of what we have discussed: it is not just one hundred, is it?"

"What? What's not a hundred?"

"You said you were carrying around one hundred extra pounds. That is not an accurate number, is it?"

"What do you do, peer into people's bathrooms? I suppose you wouldn't want to do that, if you were going to see me naked...no, you're right, it's quite a lot more than a hundred, but I don't really know how much I weigh since I put it all back on the last time. I guess I should get an accurate reading."

"Just make a practice of examining everything you say about yourself to make sure it is true, or accurate, and acknowledge when it is not or when you are not sure. Most home scales do not measure beyond three hundred, and I think you should not get on one yet. Sometimes too much truth is distracting. We do not need to know how long the road will be when we are still trying to *find* the road. Just avoid falsehoods and let the truths come naturally. Let us discover what keeping your mind on your dream does for you. We can get some scales in here and—what is it you financial people say, crunch the numbers? We can do that later, when the numbers represent victory more than defeat."

~

"Thanks for seeing me without an appointment, but I couldn't find any way of contacting you except to come here."

"That is part of my own work-elimination plan. I did have a telephone when I opened this office, but I found that most callers wanted me to tell them something magical on the telephone and then argue about it. So I had it removed. My name is Claire Spiegel. You have a dream?"

"Hi, Claire, I'm Elizabeth, very pleased to meet you. So, if I'm guessing correctly, you are a professional enabler, right? You'll work with me to identify or clarify my dream and then put steps in motion to realize it. Sort of like a life coach, but different."

"*Exactement*! You have hit the nail right on the head. With most clients, I have to drag their dream out of them, but I think you have your dream clearly ready to discuss, *non*?"

"Absolutely. I know what I want, but I wasn't sure how to get there, which is why the 'dreams made possible' line attracted me so much."

"And that would be..."

"Well, here's the awkward part: I think I know what you do, and perhaps I was able to sort it out so quickly because, well, what you do here is what I want to do."

"Your dream is to—"

"To help people make their dreams possible! I'll explain. I'd been working as a senior tax collector for the federal government for decades and I've just taken early retirement while I still had a heart and a brain—and courage, too, I suppose, to complete the trio on the yellow brick road. I thought of taking courses to be a life coach, but I think their clients' goals mostly have to do with making money. I don't want to work with people who keep me on retainer to do their thinking for them. Do you feel like you're accomplishing something personally worthwhile to you here, Claire? Are your clients' dreams worthy of your time? Do you really see dreams become possible—accomplished, even—due to your intervention?"

"Yes they are, and yes I do. Elizabeth, allow me to review what you have said: you think you want to do what I do here, correct?"

"Correct."

"That is your dream?"

"It is."

"And you are willing—prepared—to invest in this dream?"

"I am. In fact, I've looked at a lot of opportunities —courses, on-the-job training, franchises—and I know that anything worth doing will require an investment of time and money. I have some funds at my disposal."

"Elizabeth, I have—I myself have a dream. May I tell you what it is?"

"Yes, of course, if you are comfortable doing so."

"My first dream was to do exactly what I have been doing here. It is rewarding in all the ways I would wish it to be. But, as you may anticipate, I have had more than one dream. I know where there is a warm, azure sea gently touching a shore dotted with cool white buildings on a steep hillside. I have long dreamed of spending a few blissful months there, maybe longer. But I cannot be in two places so far apart at the same time. You may hold the key to that dream for me."

"It sounds beautiful there."

"Yes, it is. It will be. Now, to the business at hand. Your dream is to sit where I sit and do what I do, *n'est-ce pas*? Let us address that first. I propose that you observe my interviews for a while. I hope you are not uncomfortable in small spaces, because you will have to stay silent and unseen in that small closet over there to do it."

"Really? That would be a fabulous opportunity, Claire. Yes, please. I'm not claustrophobic, so I'll be fine in the closet, as it were. But, how shall I pay you, and how much?"

"It is quite possible that you will be my final new client for a while, and I may be your first. Each of us will sacrifice to gain. I propose you pay me ten thousand, with this condition: if we arrive at a mutually-agreeable transaction, I will keep the money and you will take over my position. If we do not, I will return all the money to you and you will find your dream elsewhere. Do you accept?"

"Although I have known you for only a few minutes, I must say that I like this arrangement a lot. The investment is very low for what I hope to achieve. Let's do it!"

~

"Kyle, can you say hello to Miss Claire? Say hello, Kyle. He can, I know he can, but he's shy of strangers, I don't blame him, poor thing, so many people don't react too well to him, but he's very well-behaved, I assure you, I saw to that. Here, Kyle, now don't touch things—'

"Excuse me. May I speak with Kyle myself, please? If he is to be my client, I must get to know him on my terms. If you would just allow us a few moments. Please, you sit there."

Fraaap!

"Holy jeez, what was that? I mean, excuse me, I didn't do that—"

"Oh, look Kyle. Your Mommy made a big whoopee! That's funny. Ha-ha-ha! Let's see if it happens when she sits again. Please be seated, Mommy."

Fraaap!

"Oh, that's funny! Now we're all laughing. That's good. Look, I had someone bring some refreshments for us today. Kyle, would you like some juice and cookies?"

"Oh, Miss, I don't think that's a good idea. He—he's so messy, aren't you Ky, you're such a spilly-pants, darlin'. But thanks."

"Here, Kyle, come sit on this blanket with me. Here's your juice."

"Be careful, Ky, don't—"

"And some juice for Miss Claire. This is like a picnic, is it not, Kyle? We are sitting on a blanket, just the two of us—oh, but Mommy could join us for some juice, okay? Mommy, come on over and sit down with us on our picnic blanket, will you, please? Good. No funny noise this time, but did you see how he was watching for it, Mummy? Now, a toast to picnics! Drink up!"

"What the hell? Oh, damn, I spilled my juice all over me—and your blanket, too. How did—? I'm so sorry."

"Oh, that is funny. Kyle thinks so, too. Look at him laughing! It was a trick glass, sorry. Ha-ha-ha. I will pay for the cleaning costs for your clothes. Do not worry about this blanket."

"Oh, my clothes are just wash and wear. But what's going on? What's your game?"

"It is a game, you are right. I have resorted to cheap parlour tricks to make a point. I will explain. But first, I have brought in a DVD player to show you something I think you will enjoy. Do you watch that 'Funny Videos' TV show? I just have a few scenes here to show you."

"No. I do like it, or did, but we don't watch it...I didn't want Ky to get any ideas about...oh my goodness, look at that cat! Look out, kitty! Oh, that's funny! Ha-ha-ha!"

"Laugh, Mommy, laugh!"

"Oh, they're really funny, aren't they, Ky? I had forgotten how funny they are. That one with the cat falling off the TV—ha-ha-ha! I can't stop laughing at it!"

"Laugh, Mommy, laugh!"

"Yes, Ky, Mommy is laughing. And you're laughing at your Mommy, silly boy!"

"It is so much fun to have fun and laugh, *n'est-ce pas*? That is all the time we have for watching it today, but I highly recommend that you and Kyle watch that show at home. And any other shows that you yourself find amusing. Not children's shows necessarily, but shows you enjoy. It will do you both a lot of good. Now, do you see what we have done?"

"We've had some laughs, but I'm not sure how that relates."

"When I asked you bring Kyle to meet me, it was so I could try to find out what is Kyle's dream that we could make possible. I had a hunch, so I prepared, as you saw. Thank you for being a good sport, but nothing that happened was an accident. Did you see how happy Kyle is when you are happy—being a good sport or silly or relaxed or imperfect, and not always his instructor or interpreter? He is a little boy, as you continually say, but that is simply a description, not his excuse, so do not let it be yours. He is a child, and he needs to be a child, not a little man, especially not a little man with a disability. Even as he must learn, he must also play. You love him deeply, and he knows that. But I believe his dream is to enjoy his mother, not just in a you-and-me-against-the-world way, but laugh-out-loud happy.

His grasp of the world around him is not very soph-isticated, but his capacity for humour is huge. You can make his dream possible by loosening your grip a bit, and laughing more. You will not need to resort to cheap tricks as I have done, but look for laughter everywhere. And learn to be happy in yourself. As Kyle matures, his liabilities will be evident enough, but his assets may not be, unless you recognize them and reward them."

"That's it? That's Ky's dream—to laugh?"

"To be precise, I think he wants to see *you* laugh. Then he can be happy and laugh too. The blind need seeing-eye dogs to see for them. Kyle needs his mother to seek laughter for him."

"Oh, I get it...I think. Like, don't fuss so much over his behaviour?"

"Correct. Many very intelligent men and women are 'spilly-pants' all their lives, you know. Kyle is just ordinary in that sense."

"Geez. It would make me so happy if he's happy. I guess it's a bit of 'you rub my back and I'll scratch yours,' eh, Kyle? I'll be happy and laugh so you can be happy and laugh, and that will make me happy. Cool! Around and around it goes! Speaking of going, I guess we better be going. How much do I owe you, Miss Claire?"

"No charge. My fee would have to be paid by Kyle, as my client, and I think he is rather unable to pay."

"Oh, are you sure? Well, gee, thanks very much. This is—this has been great. I wonder, though, if I could ask you for one more thing, a favour?"

"*Oui?*"

"Could I—could Kyle have the whoopee-cushion to take home?"

~

"What is this?"

"Mister Montcalm said for me to bring it to you this morning with his regrets, as he is unavoidably detained and unable to attend today."

"*Vraiment?* Please return this envelope to Mister Montcalm personally with this exact message: 'I will not accept this.' Here, I will write it on the envelope he has sent with you. I will expect to see him this afternoon as arranged."

~

"I don't know why I didn't do it before, on my own, you know. When I look back, I think how dumb I was not to. I guess it was just easier and cheaper to stay at home. But maybe not better."

"The wisdom of hindsight can also be a bit harsh. Ease up on yourself, Brian. You have taken action now, and you think that will work out better for you, so forget 'dumb'. You are growing up. Maturing. Taking control of your life."

"I guess I am, Miss. And you know the funniest part? My folks were glad that I wanted to move out. I thought they'd beg me to stay, maybe for the rent money or just hanging on to me, you know. They didn't. They actually helped me move out and Mom went crazy setting up my new place—and I mean that in a good way. I went back home, I mean, to my parents' place, for Sunday dinner, and you know, I can't get over how even that was different. We had lots to talk about, I guess because I hadn't been there every day. My Dad actually shook my hand when I left. My new landlady is nice, too. I have a whole basement apartment to myself—did I tell you that? Not just a bed. Got a stove and fridge and separate bedroom and all that. I've been learning to cook for myself...sort of. It's a pretty neat setup."

"And work?"

"Going real good. I'm up and on the road making calls way earlier than I used to. Got some good orders in and more coming from new accounts. And the neat thing about starting early is that I'm done earlier some days, too, and I can get out and see around the neighbourhood after I make my supper. It's pretty much out in the country, but there's a ball-field and stuff."

"Does the 'stuff' include a fire hall?"

"Yeah, how did you know? It's right next to the ball-field."

"What kind of fire department is it?"

"What kind? I don't know. Should I know? The kind that fights house fires, I guess. Schools. Churches. That's all that's out there. Why?"

"Are there words or letters on the fire hall?"

"Gosh, I don't remember. Four or five letters, I guess, over the door."

"Brian, is 'V' one of the letters?"

"'V'? Hmmm, I think maybe it is. Right! M-U-V-F-D —Mount Uniacke Volunteer Fire De- oh, hey, yeah, a volunteer fire department, just like you said, I should move to a place where they had a vol—"

"Brian?"

"Yes, Miss?"

"Join it."

~

"What did you mean, 'unacceptable'? I sent your payment over. I couldn't—it was very, very difficult for me to make it here today. I had to cut short a very important, uh, situation, but I was prepared to honour our arrangement anyway. I sent the money. What's so unacceptable about that? Don't important things ever come up for you?"

"Please do not shout, Edward. You cannot intimidate me and we must not disturb my neighbours in the other offices; we all expect quietude from each other for our various pursuits. You must never miss our meeting, Edward, because the meeting is not with me. It is with you. I am present and on time here all day. It is *you* we need here. Now that you are here I will accept payment, thank you. So, *comment ça va* with your dream?"

"I apologize for raising my voice, uh, Claire. You know, I believe you are aggravating me into a new mindset, a new paradigm. You're not afraid of me, as many people are. I represent a lot of revenue to a person like you. You don't seem to care about the money, yet you won't let me get away without paying, I'm damn certain of that. You haven't uttered one word of smarmy pop-psychology to me. You haven't given me affirmations to repeat—my mirror is so covered with little positive-thinking notes that I can hardly see myself in it, so no great loss, I guess. All psycho-babble, that's what the billion-dollar weight-loss industry has to offer, while they sell you their tasteless food so spiked with sodium that I've turned into a pillar of salt! My dog loves to lick me when I'm on a diet!"

"Your new mindset, Edward. Tell me more about that."

"Pardon me, that was crude. I'm feeling a bit light-headed, which happens this time of day. But no snacking; I'll wait until dinner. Yes, what I've been thinking is that I've been eating and drinking the quantity and quality that I was doing simply because I *could.* You know, nothing's too good for Edward King Montcalm the Second, nothing's too expensive. I don't know when that started; in my teens, I suppose. It's always been in the back of my mind, but until now I wasn't cognizant of it."

"Not at all?"

"No. Well, actually, yes, I mean, I think I—truthfully, I have not been aware of how much it was a motivator for me. 'I am a Montcalm, and I shall have whatever I want.' That has guided me in business, too, not always to my advantage."

"You mentioned that you were…I believe the term

you used was 'leveraged'?"

"Yes. Whatever I wanted I have acquired, in business investments, in my home, my toys. Travel. Food. Wines. Debts."

"Women?"

"My wife is...she puts up with me."

"Other women?"

"Do you need to ask? The pattern extends—extended—into everything. My consumption of all acquisitionable pleasures is legendary, I'm sorry to say."

"You changed to the past tense just now. Why?"

"It's that new mindset I was telling you about. This sounds like Scrooge on Christmas Day and all that, so maudlin, but one day it just came to me: I. Don't. Have to. Do that. Any. More. Like I heard the voice of the Spirit of Christmas Yet To Come. Though of course I didn't."

"You did hear a voice, though. You heard your own voice, perhaps for the first time. Not the voice of your diet counsellor or a motivational guru or a personal trainer or a psychiatrist or a hypnotist or me. Just you, Edward, talking to you, Edward. The man you want to be, speaking from inside the man you see. You faltered when you sent the courier over with my cheque, because you have been accustomed to thinking of assistance as coming from an outside agency. You cannot pay me or anyone to curb your appetites for you. You must face them yourself. You are doing that. Once you understand that, as I believe that you do now, you are well on your way to making your dream possible."

"I wish I could be confident of that. I've been at this juncture before."

"Yes, but always with a safety net that you thought was indispensable. The safety net does not teach you to walk the tight-rope. It only lures you into thinking you might try it for a few steps without risk or commitment. If you truly and honestly work at it, you can traverse any high-wire you choose to step out on, safety net or no. And hear me: any wire you *choose*. From now on, you will not choose to take every supposed pleasure that lies before you, will you? I think your true temperament might be more suited to selectivity than the consumption of everything."

"You seem to know me as well as my wife does—better, maybe. My late father was selective. Old E. K. dealt with a surgeon's precision, or a sniper's. He was a skinflint, but unarguably successful. Not as a father; he was too withholding for my needs, so I guess I grew up wanting to be different from him: successful, but less, oh, less stingy, I guess. Less remote. More engaged, more enjoying life. But I see now that I...I've ended up greedy instead. That isn't where I was headed. Jesus God, what a mess I am!"

"How does this affect the pursuit of your dream, Edward?"

"I don't know. I am confused. And hungry, a very unfamiliar sensation. I trust that I may rely on your guidance for a while yet while I sort things out?"

"You should continue to come here, yes. And you might want to clean those annoying affirmations off your mirror so you can see the whole new man who is emerging there. But there is one note you should leave. Do you know which one?"

"'A moment on the lips, a lifetime on the hips?' No, that's beneath you. 'Nothing tastes as good as being thin feels?' Oh, I don't know, there's everything there from Oprah to Bible verses. Which one should I leave, since I guess you've been in my bedroom, too?"

"'If it is to be...'"

"'...it is up to me.' The sentence with ten two-letter words that was supposed to change my life. You're saying this is the key?"

"It is a good one. You have known it all along. When you read that note tonight you will see familiar words, it's true. But you will 'get' them. You now understand."

~

"You may come out now."

"Oh, thank God! I thought I would die if I had to stay there one moment longer!"

"I apologize. It is stuffy in there, but there was no other way—"

"Oh, no worries about that, but I thought I'd give myself away when the whoopee cushion went off. Good thing you warned me, but still, that was hilarious. And it worked so well. I thought it would be corny, but not so. And that clueless young Brian, you actually had to spell it out for him, where to go for his adventure. Edward Montcalm, now, he's another type entirely, and I hope he won't outsmart himself. I look forward to working with him, if he'll continue with me. But I absolutely must tell you, Claire: you... you are fan-*tas*-tic! Where did you get your innate knowledge of what to say or do, the right thing at just the right time, or in the right way?"

"There is no right way; you know that. I often wonder what I should say next, but mostly I take my clues from the client. Focus on what they are saying, even when they do not. Especially when they do not. Many people are so scattered in their thoughts, flinging words and phrases around in a facsimile of speech, hoping someone else will give meaning to what they say. It is sad, really. They become lost in their lives. That is why this is such a good business to do."

"Well, I'm totally impressed, listening in on those sessions. Do you ever get bored, Claire, or impatient with people? You seem to treat them all with such towering respect."

"Well...I do feel impatient sometimes, with the ones who should know better, at least. But then, if they did know better they would not be here, would they? The service I provide is similar to that of an optometrist. I test their inner vision and fit them with perspectives—perspectacles, you might say— to help them inquire within themselves more clearly."

"'Perspectacles.' That's a good one! Maybe we should rename the business 'Perspectacles.'"

"I do not advise it. People have difficulty enough working out what 'Dreams Made Possible' means. But it makes just the right ones curious, so it works."

"Yes, I noticed that. I'm living proof of that, myself. So, how do we proceed?"

"Do you feel confident now to take over?"

"I'm eager, will that do? It's been my dream for such a long time to be in this sort of situation, as I told you when I first met you—consulting, counselling, that sort of thing. Helping. Steering people. So, yes, I'm very interested in taking over. What now?"

"What you have paid me to date while you have been my client and silent observer will fund my trip abroad very nicely. I had to be very careful not to steer you to do this for my reasons alone, but it does seem that our dreams coincide..."

"Absolutely! Have no fear. I wasn't pulled any more than I pushed."

"*Bon.* So. You have paid me well enough to this point. The balance of the investment required of you is your constancy. Keep doing what you have observed me doing here, in your fashion, of course. That should include using the stage-name 'Claire Speigel' and dressing conservatively, as I see you do. This has proven to work well, and will disturb ongoing clients the least. Most will not object to the change, as your manner is similar to mine—"

"Wait – what did you say? Claire Spiegel is a *nom de plume*? What...who are you, then?"

"I am 'who' you know me to be, but my name is

Manon Miroir, at least for now. The Franco-German stage name, which loosely translates to 'clear mirror', is real enough for our clients. In fact, our role will diminish in importance in their memories as they begin to direct their own affairs. In any case, you will create your own faithful clientele very quickly, I am certain, and some of mine will continue for the time necessary. So, all income, after you pay the modest expenses, will be yours now. When I run out of funds abroad I will return, and we will see then what we do next. If we both wish to continue, we will find a way to share. If one of us wishes to move on, *c'est la vie*. Agreed?"

"Absolutely. Is there a contract? Should we sign something?"

"Oh, come now, have we come this far only to—"

"Oops, sorry. I haven't back-slid, though I'll have to watch out for that. Years working in the country's biggest bureaucracy has worn certain grooves, I'm afraid."

"That is to be expected. Those grooves will fill themselves in very quickly here."

"Well, Claire-Manon, a celebration is in order. May I buy you a drink?"

"Sounds ideal, Claire-Elizabeth. I would love something strong with an olive in it as a fore-taste of my next destination. Shall we go?"

Suite 104: The Holy Ghostwriter

Hello. This is Mort. The trusted friend who gave you this number believes you would benefit from my assistance, and therefore you will receive it. I know you feel it's urgent. After the beep, please state your first name only, no titles or affiliations, and a telephone number where I can reach you on Monday morning. You will have only two minutes to describe your concerns on this recording. Please take comfort from knowing that many have been where you are now, and that there is a remedy for every situation, and for all faiths and doctrines. Everything is in confidence. Go in peace.

"Yes, hello, this is Reverend...oh, sorry, I forgot. Hello, this is Bob...just Bob, right. Thank you for taking my call, I mean, thank you for listening to this message. Oh yes—the phone number in my study is 555-9744. I think I really need your help. I've just experienced one of the worst—no, *the* worst Sunday of my career.

At this point—it's late Sunday night now—I don't think I can face another Sunday, not as the spiritual leader of First—of my particular flock, anyway.

"A clergy friend directed me to you. Said you were of immense help to him a few months back. You must have been because I didn't even know that he was experiencing—uh—difficulties. It's just that, oh, I know this may sound dramatic, but it seems all of a sudden the bottom has fallen right out of my faith. I've lost my foundation and I'm not certain how firm it ever was. I don't just mean that I'm questioning some of the more, um, *challenging* elements of our creed, though I am doing that, but this morning as I stood in the pulpit, with a sermon all written and re-hearsed, scriptures selected and hymns chosen, I felt totally lost. Lost. I felt as if I were a great imposter standing up there. I was the devil quoting Scripture. Surely people can see right through me. There are people in my congregation whose faith could move mountains—literally. I...I don't have the faith of a mustard seed. I don't see how I can carry on that charade. I disgust myself, you know that? People could see that something was wrong. The choir knew, for sure. I had to leave the pulpit during the fi-nal hymn to collect myself, and barely made it back in time for the bene—" *Beep*.

The Very Reverend Mortimer Evers, Archbishop Emeritus of the Diocese of Halifax, now supply rector of tiny Saint Jude and All the Saints and Chap-lain at the Memorial Hospital, both in the seaside town of South River, wrote down the names and phone numbers of this and two more callers, listening intently to each message.

Then, carefully and deliberately, Mort Evers pressed the *Erase* button on his desktop answering machine, waiting until the machine beeped the signal that its memory was erased and it was ready to listen again.

He studied the three names and numbers. He hadn't made any notes from their messages. He would remember as he called them, although—and he sighed as he thought this thought—their complaints were all similar, variations on a theme. Always a crisis of faith, no matter what road they travelled to get there or what it was they had lost their faith in. A hellishly busy week saving souls. Or helping parishioners deal with family crises. Or finding enough money to heat the church in the winter. Topped off by a lousy Sunday morning caused by thoughtless criticism from a congregation leader. It could all lead to a pastor's Sunday evening of quiet desperation. He or she would call a friend, usually another member of the clergy, sometimes a trusted lay person not always of their faith or any faith, to confess their worst sin: the sin of being fed up with their congregation, or of disbelief, or at least of not remembering how to believe, whether in the Deity or in themselves. The sin of not believing in sin.

Mort knew it was terrifying for these ministers. Their income and position in the community depended on what they believed more than on what they knew how to do or how well they did it. He'd been there. He was sometimes there still, but he was no longer frightened when he became overwhelmed and occasionally lost sight of the ideal.

These days, Mort would have to stop and consider if you asked him how his faith was. Was it cloudy or fair, midnight or noon? He had learned that those were merely theological meteorological conditions. Whether he was in the clutch of doubt or the slippery grip of certainty, if he waited five minutes it could change.

What Mort Evers had learned, and which comforted him greatly, was that what he believed or didn't quite believe in any given moment didn't hinder his ability to minister to his flock. When they prayed with fervour, he surrounded them with words that protected them from doubt. When they doubted their creed, he encouraged them to examine the roots of that doubt with vigour.

In all cases, he urged them to be easy on themselves, to allow frightening thoughts that entered their minds to wander round and maybe wander off, to widen their path so they could wobble a bit and still be on it. He surprised everyone with his non-judgmental approach and his ability—as tall and thin as he was—to walk in their shoes even while they were still in them.

~

"Good morning. May I speak with Bob, please?"

"This is Bob."

"I received your message this morning. This is Mort."

"Oh, Mort, thank God you called. I've been waiting, hoping you would call. I've had one hell of a night, pardon my language—"

"No pardon needed. That is probably the proper word to describe how you're feeling. Now here's—"

"My God, Mort, what am I going to do? I'm such a fraud, and—"

"Bob, listen to me, now." Mort Evers' voice was as deep as a farm well, and carried a promise of green pastures and still waters in it. "This call will be of necessity short. My message for you this morning is two-fold, Bob. First, I can and I will help you. Second, I assure you that next Sunday, and all your duties between now and then, will go much better than they have recently. Will you take my word for it, Bob?"

"I guess I'll have to, won't I? But won't that be dishonest? I'm not feeling very...faithful these days, and I'm—oh, damn, I'd forgotten, I'm supposed to lead a men's prayer breakfast tomorrow morning, too!" Bob groaned.

"Bob, listen to me please, listen very carefully. First, I can and will help you. Second, you haven't lost your faith. You've lost your way. There is a difference. Do you understand me?"

"No," Bob said. He sounded like he was not interested in understanding.

Mort marvelled at how people become entrenched in the very thoughts that give them the most grief. He made a mental note to use that in an address when next invited to give one.

"Yes, you do," Mort said. "Do you watch the movies, Bob?"

"What? Yes, some. Why?"

"Have you seen *Lord of the Rings*, any of them?"

"Well, yes, I don't know which ones, they all seem the same, and a bit blasphemous, with their magic and wizards and super-powers."

"If you have lost your faith, Bob, what do you care about blasphemy?" Mort asked with a chuckle.

"*Touché*. I don't know what I believe right now. That was then."

"Agreed. Forgive my poor attempt at humour. Bob, in those movies, do the hobbits get lost?"

"The hobbits? Um, sure, those little people are getting lost all the time. One of them, whosis, Samwise, is it, he can't go anywhere unless he's had a snack, and they're always being led astray by that evil cave creature, oh..."

"Gollum," said Mort, his voice sounding like he was in a cave himself. "Right you are. Now, Bob, still in the movie, when the little hobbits have wandered off their path, where is Sauron, the big bad guy?"

"Gosh, if I had known I was going to get quizzed on movie trivia I would have paid closer attention," Bob said. "Where was Sauron? Umm, let me see... Middle Earth? The Firth of Forth? I don't know, Mort, the language of the whole series was pretty impenetrable to me, with so many place names and alliances and tribal battles. Sounds like the Old Testament, but worse. Why are we—?"

"Bob, would you say, while the hobbits were running through the swamps and caves and having snacks on the road to Mordor, that Sauron was still there in Mordor?"

"Are you sure it's Sauron? I keep thinking Valdemort."

"Nope, sorry, different series. Similar, though, now that you mention it. It is confusing."

"I thought it was just me. So, okay, sure. Sauron was still in Mordor, because once in a while they had some evidence that he could...he could see them... even when they were lost..."

Bob's voice trailed off into silence. Mort waited.

"Could you repeat your question, please?" Bob finally said.

"Certainly. I said that you have not lost your faith, but that you have lost your way. And I asked if you knew the difference."

Bob exhaled into the phone mouthpiece. "I might, Mort. I might. You're saying that God is still there, can see me, but I have gone where I can't see Him? I'm just lost in a swamp or a cave?"

"Does that encourage you?"

"Well, yes, it does actually, weird as that sounds. Yesterday morning, I don't know what brought this on, really I don't. Maybe many things, like some conversations in the choir room before we went in, scornful jokes about faith from people I wouldn't have expected...but I suddenly had this awful feeling that all the things I had believed in since I was a child were all gone, false, never happened, you know? I felt so *bereft*. It was awful, as I told you in my message last night. I loved it when I was in my faith, right? Like really solidly in my convictions. It's such a comfort to be there and feel that. But I felt like it had all fallen away, and I—I just cried. That's what I did last night. I cried. My wife didn't know what to do with me."

"Bob, here's what I want you to keep foremost in your thoughts until we meet later this week: your grief is your hope. Can you remember that? *My grief is my hope*. Write it down. You were grieving the loss of your faith when you hadn't lost your faith at all, you had just lost sight of that in which you have your faith. Interference with the signal, you might call it. If you didn't care, you wouldn't grieve. Therefore, have faith in your grief, as it will lead you to reconnect with the signal and carry on. Got that?"

"Y-yes...I'm just writing it here, 'my grief is...' I'm sorry, can you say it again? I didn't sleep at all last night and I'm pretty strung out right now."

Mort Evers repeated the five words slowly, and Bob slowly wrote them down.

"Good, Bob," Mort said. "You know, you might find something in that to say to your prayer breakfast to-morrow. Don't assume they are all rock-solid in their faith and are simply there to practice their cheer-leading. They're just ordinary men who are willing to get up early to meet downtown for breakfast. Sit beside them, figuratively speaking, and talk honestly to them about how holding on to faith is sometimes hard. They'll thank you for that. Being a person of faith is like being a recovered alcoholic: you are never safe. That's why we have churches. D'you see, Bob?"

"Maybe I do. I should say it sounds cynical, but I can't find fault with what you say at all, not this morning, anyway."

"Don't dig too hard, Bob," Mort said. "This week especially, you should ignore whatever doesn't work for you. Now, my service includes a personal encounter between us later this week, at which time I will give you your sermon for next Sunday, so you'll have a little space in which to gather yourself together. Is there any special scripture or theme you have been speaking on that I should know about?"

The two clerics discussed the details and arranged their rendezvous.

"Now I must give you my office location, so please concentrate on writing down the address correctly," Mort said. "The entrance is hard to find, but it really is there, just like your faith. You may be standing right outside the door and still wonder if you are lost."

There wasn't a voice that could smile through a telephone line better than Mort Evers'.

"Thank you so much, Mort," Bob said. "I believe God has heard my cries and sent you to me. I know that sounds odd, having said what I said, but old habits and all that. So, listen, will you be sending me a bill for your services, or how do you want to handle that?"

"I'll explain the method of payment when we meet on Thursday. And remember, everything is confidential, so I will appreciate your not divulging my service or location to anyone. Which means you must come alone, of course. Be of good cheer, Bob."

Mort hung up and entered Bob's appointment in his datebook, then wrote a reminder in his notebook: *Address topic - why are people so entrenched in the ideas that give them the most grief?*

~

"Good morning! You must be Helen!"

It was said that Mort Evers could make even his enemies feel welcome, though no one would believe that he had enemies. Mort would say that even Our Lord had welcomed Judas to supper that fateful night, making his telling of the Last Supper sound more like the opening of an Agatha Christie novel. He would add that the Old Testament noted that we may entertain angels unaware, so better to be safe than sorry.

"Yes, I'm Reverend Helen. Are you Mort? Oh, my! You—you're the Arch—"

"I'm just Mort, and let me tell you what a pleasure it is to meet you, Helen," he boomed, showing her into the little office. "I'm always curious about young people in the ministry today. In my time, which I confess was over half a century ago, you could say that people almost expected one to join the clergy if one showed a strong faith. Nowadays, not so much. Would you say that is so, Helen?"

"What's that, You—I mean—Mort?"

"Don't be nervous, my dear. I was just wondering if you went into the clergy against the expectations of your peers, or your family?"

"N-no, I don't know. Do you know my family?" Helen asked.

"I don't think so," Mort said, "and I would prefer not to know if I do, unless it affects our work together in some material way."

"I suppose it doesn't matter," Helen said. "Nothing I say matters. That's why I called you. I work so hard, but nobody pays any attention to me. The church officials meet without me or override me, the organist picks hymns on her own without consulting me about the message I will preach, the children's groups are just chaos. Do you know, on Sunday morning, maybe I told you this already, they were talking during my sermon? The congregation were talking amongst themselves. Out loud. *In church*!"

"Yes, my dear, you did tell me that. Please sit down and let's see if we can figure out how to get your flock of sheep to obey their shepherd." He folded his remarkably long and remarkably thin self into a chair behind his desk.

"Oh, well, I wouldn't say I want them to obey me," Helen began.

"Then what would you have them do, child?" Mort asked.

"Well, I— I would have them follow..."

"Follow whom, may I ask?"

"Well, follow...follow the, uh, the teachings of, uh...Jesus."

"That wasn't so bad to say, was it? Now, I'm curious, Helen. What does Jesus teach about hymns, exactly?"

"What?"

"Did Our Lord mention hymns in His teachings, that your organist could be reminded of His Holy Word on that subject?"

"No, of course not, I just—"

"Ah." Mort leaned back in his creaky chair. "Then I wonder if he said something about how your Official Board members should behave?"

"No, but—"

"How about congregations chatting when you preach?"

"What? No! Well, all right, yes He did: 'Those who have ears to hear, let them hear.' Listen, I don't think it helps to mock the teachings of Jesus. Of course He didn't speak about these mundane or modern things. I just expected, as spiritual leader of my congregation, they would want me to lead them, well, spiritually."

"You want your flock to know they are your sheep?"

"Well, I suppose so. I want them to know that God loved them so much that He gave His only Son—"

"Yes, yes, that's what we all want. But Helen, if you expected to find such people in your congregation, already fully formed in their faith, you were seriously misled in Divinity School. If they are not there, the born-again faithful, it's your mission to create them. You have to turn your assorted free-range livestock into your flock of faithful sheep, fat and happy in God's green pastures under your protection. That's your job."

"But how? They don't even listen to me. The only people who came to shake my hand at the end of the service yesterday were people who can't go out the other doors because they're in wheelchairs!" Helen's chin crumpled and tears welled in her eyes.

"Helen," Mort said as he passed the tissue box he kept handy, "do you have a pet?"

"Pet?"

"Yes, you know, a cat or dog? A budgie, perhaps? An angel-fish?"

"No, I—I didn't think the Manse Committee would approve of a pet."

"Ah, the dreaded Manse Committee. Did you have a pet as a child?"

"Oh, yes, we had several dogs on our farm. I'm from Out West, and my family had a large farm there for generations. We always had dogs. Cats, too, but they were barn cats, mousers, not pets. The dogs were like farm hands, really, herding the cattle—"

"Really? Tell me about them."

"The border collies were my favourite, and when my brothers and I were very small, they would herd us, too, Mother said, just like the cows, rounding us up if we wandered off..."

Mort allowed the mental image Helen was viewing to sharpen, and then prompted her again.

"Were they friendly, these dogs? Did they bark? Or bite?"

"Oh, they were gentle as lambs around us. One especially, Doogie, we called him. I loved him, I really did. He was with us a long time. All my life while I was growing up at home, in fact. He died while I was at Divinity College, that first year. My father took it hard, and so did I. You should have seen Doogie, flying around those heavy hooves, nipping and barking to get the cattle to stay in the herd."

Helen's eyes glistened as she spoke, then she met his gaze. "No, to answer your question. He didn't bite. None of the dogs did, certainly not us and not the cattle, either. They looked as though they would, though, baring their teeth when they were working the herd. And you know, no matter how long the cattle were in that herd, they always believed that the dogs would bite them *this* time, isn't that funny? They always ran from them, anyway. The collies did it all with their barking and posture. It was marvellous to watch."

"Do you think you could learn that?" Mort asked.

"What? To bark? You want me to *bark* at my congregation?"

"Wouldn't that be a hoot?" Mort threw his head back in a great laugh. "Instead of the Invocation, you'd mount the pulpit and start barking like Old Yeller! Ah-ha-ha!"

He was tickled with his imagery. Helen was not. She stood to leave. "I'm sorry, Mort. I was told on good authority that you—"

"Oh, sit, child, sit," Mort said, recovering. "Never miss the opportunity to find humour in your serious quest to save souls. No, I do not suggest that you begin your service of worship by barking, though some day it might appeal to you. Tempting as that idea may be, let's move on to what you can do to get those wandering bovines or ovines of yours to become a flock. They do want to be in one, you know. They don't want to be eaten by wolves, do they?"

"No."

"No. So, let's see if we can show them a dog so effective that they will crowd around you for dear life."

"What, like a pit bull? I would never—"

"No, I was thinking about a collie, since that's what you're used to. A collie pup. Yes, a soft little pup as young as is feasible to take from its mother. You must get yourself a puppy, Helen. And you must take the dear wee thing with you everywhere except into the sanctuary. Well, no, maybe I speak too soon. Does your congregation have a Blessing of the Animals?"

"A what? No. I've not heard of it. Is it scriptural?"

"Oh, free your head from the Good Book. Live in the world! Look around you! You can bless anything you like. The fishing towns on this treacherous ocean coast have been blessing their fleets for eons, as well they should, since not all of the fishers who go down to the sea in ships come back to their families alive. Several churches bless the animals, with everyone bringing in their cats and dogs, and birds, no doubt, maybe mice or reptiles, though I can't imagine the predators and prey all mixed together, but Noah managed it in the Ark, didn't he? Oh yes, and one pastor even had a blessing of the—whatchamac-allits—these bleepy things everyone carries now."

He pulled a phone from his cardigan pocket and set it on his desk. "That pastor had his head on right that day. And, since you mention it, there is much in Scripture to back up these blessings."

"Such as?"

"Oh, such as Psalm 8. The poet is praising God for the heavens, all sheep and oxen, yea, and the beasts of the field, et cetera, et cetera. So, there's your blessing of the animals, good to give thanks for all that. But animals were pretty much all there was in those days for food, transportation, clothing. Just sheep. No big-screen TVs, no cellular things." He pointed to the phone. "If these had been invented, the Psalmist would have had a very long list to sing God's praises about. The Good Book would be much, much longer."

Helen was silent. Mort took advantage of the pause to make a short entry in his notebook under the previous speech title: *What was in the Psalmist's Pockets: do we have more to give thanks for now than he did?*

Helen said, "I don't know if I know what I'm supposed to do now."

"You will continue to be your own sweet self," Mort replied. "But you need some lessons on how to get your flock to behave the way they themselves want to behave. So you shall find yourself a new puppy, and that puppy will teach you all you need to know. The children will be obedient all day long if they know they can hold your puppy afterwards. Maybe you'll let them name it for you. Everyone in the congregation will ask you about it though they may have found it difficult to inquire about you yourself. And you must limit yourself to just one amusing anecdote per inquiry; if they want to know more, they can ask you again later, maybe invite you over for tea to show you their beloved cat or budgie or prized African violet. You will, of course, tell your Manse Committee that you think their no-dog rule is silly, if they mention it, as it is your home, but you will take full responsibility for any puppy accidents. As soon as the pup is old enough, you must take it to obedience class, so you can learn what the dog needs from you for a happy life. They'll teach you there that being affirmative and consistent is the best way to show animals—and people—that you care. Does that make sense?"

"Yes, when you say it. It does. You really mean I could have a dog here, at home? It would make that big old manse seem a lot less—"

"Less lonely? It surely would. Anything you can do to populate your accommodation with positive energy is good. You should know that even those of us with busy, loving families around us have found the manse or glebe to be very, very lonely at times. Gather your supporters where you can, Helen. A collie pup is a great place to start. As the bumper sticker says, the best things in life are furry."

Smiling at his joke, Mort picked up a brown envelope with HELEN written on it and handed it to her.

"What's this?"

"This is your sermon for this Sunday, complete with scripture references and hymns. Just part of my service, ma'am." He touched the brim of an imaginary hat.

"Thank-you very—oh, hymns? But it's Thursday morning, and the organist has already—"

"Helen. You are the shepherd, and you must shep. Tell the organist to rehearse these hymns with the choir this evening. Period. Then announce 'em on Sunday. What else will she play? They'll know them anyway. These are old favourites. That's a trick you must never forget, by the way: when you feel you are in the doghouse with your congregation, so to speak, give them the old chestnuts to sing and tell the organist to keep the pedal to the metal. They will forgive anything if you do that."

"Oh dear. Are you sure? Well, of course you are, you have so much more experience than I...and I did ask for help. I'm just not...what's the text of this—of my sermon this Sunday?"

"The Beatitudes. Blessed are the meek, and the others."

"The meek? But I thought you were counselling me to step up and—and bark! Now you want me to preach meekness?"

Mort lifted his hands in mock surrender. "Look at you, you're coming out of your shell already! No, my sister, I am not asking you to preach meekness. The Beatitudes are one of the most misinterpreted sections of the misunderstood Gospels. Why do you suppose Christ took the time to bless those with quiet personality attributes on that sunny hillside that day? Do you think He meant to bless *only* the meek, *only* the peacemakers, *only* the poor? Do you think that He meant *not* to bless—and instead to condemn—the deal-makers, the busy entrepreneur who employs everyone, the strong, and the brave? The Old Testament is full of stories of heroes with just those qualities. Jesus wouldn't have said, but didn't say, that they should be condemned, though He was a bit down on the wealthy, I will admit. No. That sermon was to give the meek their due, and the poor and so on, because they *also* have their place and the strong should not run over them. But by its very omission He must also have been saying that leadership is such a blessed quality that it need not be pointed out."

He sighed. "Except to you, today. Sometimes one needs a reminder of the obvious, the thing not said. After all, Jesus didn't write His own How-To Book, did He? When this was all written down a few hundred years later, the miraculous, wonderful things He said were what people remembered. They left out the obvious, and now people overlook it or assume he never said it at all.."

As Mort wrote in his notebook: *Did God assume we'd know what He had left out of the Gospel?* his device buzzed on his desk.

"Time's almost up, I'm afraid. I have another visitor in a few minutes and I don't want you two to meet in the elevator. Now, about my fee."

"Yes, please, I will pay you, of course." Helen reached for her purse.

"Sorry, you cannot pay me. You must tell no one of your visit here, except your dog, in whom you can confide all things, trust all things, believe all things. I repeat, tell no one of your encounters with me this week. The person who gave you my phone number does not expect you to report back. She or he will simply expect to see you happier in your work, as I think you will be. You do have a fine sermon there, if I do say so myself. I hope you will deliver it with a performance that would make your Homiletics professor proud, and you must accept the credit for it, or give God the glory, but not me. It's not a lie, not even a white one; you took this step to seek help, and that sermon is the result of your effort."

"Then how can I pay you back?" Helen asked. "It wouldn't feel right not to."

"Here's how it works," Mort said. "You can pay it forward, as the saying goes. Someday in the future, one of your colleagues will find him- or herself in the valley of the shadow of one bogeyman or another. The standards of faith that we and our colleagues of the cloth hold ourselves to are quite unreasonable, so we frequently feel we have failed. When you get that call, you'll use your good judgment. Is this just a bad day for your friend? Is she or he in a disagreement of his or her own making, which most adults encounter frequently and have to extricate themselves from—especially adults in charge of the social and religious activities of a group of 150 or so families?"

"That many?" Helen said. "I wish I had that problem."

"You will, my dear, you will, especially if you deliver this sermon with some energy, some spice, like the farm girl you are. Pitch it to them like you pitched forkfuls of manure out of your barn. Anyway, if the causes of your colleague's future distress are temporal and temporary, offer them your own counsel or not, as you see fit. But if your friend is facing a dark night of the soul, and you feel that self-help, or prayer, or your intervention may not be sufficient to pop them out of it, give them my number and encourage them to call me. You'll remember the rest of the instructions, because this is how it worked for you. First, it will be a Sunday night, and—"

"How do you know that?"

"Simple. In most Christian traditions, Sunday is the end of the week. Seventh day and all that. For us clergy, it's show-time and payday, all wrapped into one. Your next week will live or die by the degree to which you have portrayed faith, hope and charity in church, and whether you have had a good pastoral prayer and great hymns. Sunday night in our business is like Friday night for a stock broker. If it's been a bad week, it's at its worst on Friday for him. You called me Sunday night. They all do. I come in on Monday morning to retrieve the calls."

"I didn't know I was following a formula," Helen said. "I don't know whether to be ashamed or comforted by that."

"Take your pick," Mort said, "but I would always choose comfort where I can. True, sometimes a call comes in on a weekday, but I am not able to respond to those. I just deal with the Sunday night specials. We talk on Monday morning, as you and I did, while the caller is still fresh with despair, and I try to give some perspective on the caller's weakened state."

"It sounds a bit, well, a bit formulaic, but that is what happened, and you certainly have helped me feel better, Mort. I felt so alone and helpless..."

Mort laughed. "There are times and places for the *sanctum sanctorum*, but when you're down and out, a good swift kick in the catechism is what you need to get you back in your preferred groove. I am God's self-appointed creed-kicker."

"Oh, goodness!" Helen said. "You speak so...so boldly. I don't think I could ever—"

"You don't have to be me. You just have to be you. I think there is a Helen inside you that perhaps even you have not met yet. Perhaps God knows that Helen, and God will send you a collie pup to introduce her to you and the rest of the world. Now let me finish: your sad friend will call me on a Sunday night, we will talk on Monday morning and then meet later in the week. You must not follow up with your friend after that occasion, as your referrer will not follow up with you now. That conversation would be too awkward."

"How do you mean?"

"Well, how does this sound: 'How's your faith, sister Helen, still weak?' 'Oh, it's coming along, I guess, but still feeble.' See what I mean? Trust me on this, we leaders of the Lord's flocks would rather discuss our urinary tract infections than our wobbly faith. Hence, the occasional need for my services."

"I'm to pay it forward, then."

"Yes, you likely will be called upon to do that one day. You won't have to go looking for an opportunity. It will come along, but please do your best to screen out all but the most wretched."

"I will. I will. I am so, so grateful to you for all you have done for me, Mort, thank you so very much."

"You are welcome, my dear. But when that pup has widdled on some donated heirloom carpet in the manse that should have been tossed a century ago, just remember how grateful you are today. Now, scoot. My eleven o'clock will be on their way up."

"I hope we'll meet again."

"Perhaps we will, Helen. And you can count on this: after a half-century of learning the names of hundreds, nay, thousands of parishioners and their families, it's all a blur to me now, so when we meet again, I assure you I won't recognize you. And don't remind me. That way we can start afresh. I look forward to meeting you sometime. Now go in peace."

~

"Mort, it's Linda."

"Linda, my love, how are you and—?" Linda was one of Mort's favourite clerics. She had answered the call, as they say, after years in a different career, and had brought no illusions with her.

"Good. Listen, Mort, something serious has happened—"

"Oh, God, Linda, are you—?"

"I'm fine, Mort. It's Father Kevin, a friend of a friend, a Catholic priest. He's in a very bad way and none of us can...well, we all feel that you are the man to help him, or to help us to help him. It's very bad."

"Now, Linda, you know the protocol. He—"

"Yes, I do, but I—we all think this is an exceptional case. You'll likely find your answering machine filled with messages from some of your alumni on his behalf, but we realized tonight that we shouldn't wait until you come in next Monday to hear them. May I please tell you what's going on?"

"Of course. Shoot."

"You know that missing person case, the young woman whose body they just found in the woods?"

"She was the mother of a young child, if I'm not mistaken? So very tragic. Yes, I did hear that."

"Well, hear this. The police took her husband to the station after they found his wife's body. Her brother heard about it and he went to the station so he could be there to support his brother-in-law, I guess. It has been such an awful time for her whole family."

"I can imagine it was. Go on."

"So her brother arrives at the station, and waits and waits for his brother-in-law to come in. And he doesn't come in. Finally, he goes to the front desk and says where the heck is my brother-in-law, Mr So-and-so. And they take him into a back room and then they tell him."

"And what do they tell him, Linda?"

"That he confessed to her murder. The husband. No surprise, really, is it? Apparently he confessed on the way to the station. They had evidence of poison, I think. I guess it was grisly to find and an excruciating death for her. I don't think that's hit the news media yet."

"That tragedy just continues to deepen. So how —?"

"The brother is Father Kevin, the priest. He has gone right off his rocker, right over the deep end, as you might expect. He threatened to kill his brother-in-law, right in the police station, I guess. They didn't charge him for that, but only because someone from the diocese came and got him."

"Where is he now?"

"He's home, in his Glebe, but nobody wants to leave him alone. He's screaming bloody murder and revenge, and they had to drag him out of the sanctuary after he went in to celebrate mass and smashed quite a bit of stuff there. I—Mort, I just stepped out from there to call you. I know he'll need medical help too, but I think he's—"

"Possessed by demons? Yes, he is, Linda. No doubt about it. No need to hesitate about that. This can easily transpire when one is wounded so deeply. We all have this in us, as you well know, and when the goodness and charity we so earnestly cloak ourselves in suddenly gets whipped off, we have no defences ready against our darker selves. Oh, he is in such agony now."

"It's hurting us all. You know, to see him, to hear him in an agony of faith like that, it truly shakes you, no matter what affiliation. He was in the sanctuary, screaming at God for the loss of his sister—I guess she was his twin, too—and for losing his brother-in-law, whom he loved and now hates. Terrifying, truly. Everyone's in tears."

"His twin sister. Cruelty upon cruelty." Mort paused, and then asked, "What would you have me do?"

"Can you come into the city, Mort? Right now, I mean? I know it's a long drive and it's late, but the weather's clear—"

"Of course I will. I can call a friend to drive me. That's what it's all about, isn't it? Friends, helping friends. Some days go very badly, don't they, and we need help from so many sources, temporal and eternal, to get through them. Many of my most fervent prayers are simply for tomorrow to come quickly, just help us find a way to make it to tomorrow, and then to the day after that. Pain seems to ease with time, the demons lose their strength and the angels of faith and reason return..."

Mort's voice trailed off. Linda waited a moment, then said, "Mort?"

"Amen. I thought I had better pray just then. Prayer might get pushed aside for later in the fog of war, mightn't it? Now, you want me to come to town, and then what?"

"Come to the Glebe on Green Street. We just need you to be with us, Mort, to help us while we are struggling to help Father Kevin. Or maybe you would speak to Kevin directly? Whatever you think best. I thought you should know, everyone's asking for you. You're not as unknown as you'd like to think. You're known as The Sermonator by the grateful many."

"Don't tell me that," Mort said. "I like my invisibility the way I imagine it. Tell me, has his Archbishop been called?"

"The Archbishop? Gosh, no, we were trying to keep this from the higher-ups. Wouldn't they have to suspend him if he's threatening to kill someone?"

"Hmmm. Just a minute—yes, here it is. Call this number, Linda, and tell the Archbishop, the emeritus, not the presiding, that you are calling at my request. Just say Mort asked you to call. Tell him to meet me outside the church. Oh, and send any laity home. No doubt someone has brought food. We'll want it eventually, I'm sure. They can leave it in the Glebe. Tell the Archbishop to stay in his car until I arrive, which should be in about an hour and a quarter, if my driver hasn't gone to bed. If he has, it will be an hour and sixteen minutes."

"Okay, I'll call him as soon as we hang up."

"Oh, tell him to bring Rinpoche too, if he's in the country."

"The Buddhist leader?"

"Yes. Tell them it's Code Purple. Got that?"

"Code Purple? You guys have colour-coded

alarms? Are you kidding me?"

Mort chuckled. "Code Purple was the Arch-bishop's idea. It means that there is a real and present danger that could harm the shepherds and flocks of all stripes under our care, and we must intervene in a concerted effort to turn this unholy mess into a saving grace. The priest who hates his brother-in-law and God, and hates himself more for hating them, will know that we, the church's highest representatives in these parts, know how he feels and are cool with it. Wild fears quickly follow such loathing. We need to dispel them both 'PDQ' for our brother Kevin so he can regain his rational mind. Rinpoche will likely take the lead this time. He has some wonderful things to say about loss. Oh, what does he call it? Sam...*sansara*, that's it: sansara, the cycle of loss. They'll both come if they are at all able."

"And get Kevin to forgive his brother-in-law?"

"Would you? Would I? That's a huge burden we lay upon the wronged and the oppressed. He can plan to hate him for the rest of his life if he finds comfort and reason in that tonight, and he may change his mind later. Right now we need to help him find his mind. We'll discuss this more one day soon, you and I. Do you have anything left in that case of Malbec you were telling me about?"

"Sure do, and you know I'd love to discover what wisdom is in those bottles, under your guidance."

"I'm so easily distracted, aren't I, thinking of great wine and conversation. Now, Linda, you wait near the entrance of the church and watch for me so I can get an update from you when I arrive. I hope I'll be in a sporty little two-seater—I'll ask my driver for it. You've done well. Thank you for breaking the rules to call me. Now go in peace."

Mort called his driver-friend. No, he wasn't in bed yet. Yes, he could be at the door in mere minutes. Yes, in the sports car. If the Mounties stopped them for speeding, the sight of the gowned cleric folded up inside the tiny car would surely accord them nothing worse than a warning, and perhaps an escort.

The Right Reverend Mortimer Evers quickly donned his ceremonial garb, kissed his wife good-night, and waited by the front door for his ride. As he prepared to spend the night wrestling with demons, he laughed to himself.

"The Sermonator," he murmured. "I like that."

Suite 105: The Flower Painter

Dearest Mae -

The *awfullest* thing has happened to me!

I tripped on the edge of the mat by my back door —it's been there forever, don't know why it suddenly leaped up and caught the toe of my slippers on Sunday morning as I was about to let Puss in, or out, can't remember which now, but the next thing I knew I was knickers over tea-kettle on the floor!

To add injury to insult, I reached out to break my fall—instinct, you know—not thinking that I might break my arm and put myself out of work, just like that! Fortunately, I stumbled ahead enough to catch the edge of the kitchen counter, and thus slowed my fall but—alas!—I badly sprained my shoulder on the way down.

I suppose I shouldn't complain, as I have no broken bones—not like poor Cassie did and you know what happened to her, so quickly, too—but my left arm is all strapped up in the most uncomfortable way, and "Dr" says I mustn't move it at all—NOT EVEN TO DRESS! I do think he is being a bit extreme, but since I can't undo the straitjacket he put on me,

I'll have to live with it. I tried to wiggle out of it when I got home, but didn't like how that felt so I guess I'll have to acquiesce until it heals. I wonder if he put it on the right way, you know how the young "Drs" can be, so quick.

All because of that dratted cat! Puss had best watch where he goes in the next while, in case the toe of my shoe finds him!

But the worst thing is that I can do nothing that requires two hands. I can still paint, thank goodness, with some difficulty, but I can't manoeuvre the heavy cases from Montreal, so I must make sure I am in my studio when they deliver them, which is 'anytime between 8:00 a.m. and 4:00 p.m.' and by anytime they mean *any*time! How frustrating! That's very poor customer service, I told them, but they have no concern for how I am to cope, it's all about *their* convenience.

Ah well, no sense going on about it, nothing you or I can do but our best in the circumstances, as Father would say. Though I don't know what these circumstances will bring.

Hope all is well with you and that your tests come back with good results. I hope hospitals in Scotland have improved their hygiene since we were young. Miss you.

Your loving sister,
Bella

~

Dear Mrs. Legère:

I have suffered a bit of an accident and my left arm is to be strapped up immobile for a few weeks, so "Dr" says.

As you may recall, I go to my studio on Barrington Street to paint three days each week, and some of my work there just absolutely needs two good hands.

I wonder if you would permit your daughter to come to help me after school until my injury is healed? I will have to teach her how to do the tasks —opening cases that are delivered, re-packing them to send off to my distributor, cleaning my brushes, etc. I would pay her, of course, if required.

Wouldn't ask if I didn't really need the help.

Hope to hear from you soonest,

Bella Hilchey (your neighbour at #6268)

~

From: Rochelle Legère (bellechelle@notmail.com)
To: Celine Gaultier (lineisfine@noodle.com)
Subject: MONEY!!!

Hey Celine guess what???????

I got a job after school, 3 jours par semaine!!! It's just temporary. An old lady that lives in the apartments at the end of our street broke her arm and she's some kind of artist and needs me to help her. I told Maman that I wouldn't do it if I didn't like it but she goes you wanted money and you're too young for Mickey Dee's so try it. Its only minimum wage but maybe I'll get enough to buy a ticket outta here LOL

    Chelle

~

Dear Mr. Fong:

I regret to inform you that I have injured my left arm (not my painting arm) in a small accident. I am still able to paint as well as before, quality is not affected, but I cannot do some tasks quite as quickly, so I may have to slow 'production' a bit for a few weeks.

I think you should continue to send the same number of vases and plates in each shipment, as that number works best for packing, but I may require more time returning each completed order. I know this means you won't have as many finished units to send to your stores for a while. This is so unfortunate, as you have said my vases seem to be coming back into popularity just now. I do regret this inconvenience.

I will resume my usual 'output' just as soon as I can.

    Yours truly,

    B. Hilchey

P.S. I believe it is my new 'tropicals' line that have spurred the new attention, in addition to the dear old-fashioned garden flowers of my youth. Believe it or not, those Bird of Paradise and Hibiscus flowers are easier to paint than chrysanthemums or gladioli, don't ask me why. BH

~

From: Rochelle Legère (bellechelle@notmail.com)
To: Celine Gaultier (lineisfine@noodle.com)
Subject: IT'S A DUMP!!!

OMG Celine you should see where I go to work! The old lady works in a crappy old building on this street downtown, near where my mother works, but I never saw this place before. It's a dumpy little building, and so is she. Not my mother LOL. The old lady I mean. Her name is Missus Hilchee I think. Sounds Chinese. She has some kinda accent, but she's not Chinese, not like my friends at school anyway. Not francais either. She paints flowers on these glass bottles or whatever. That's all she does. She does like six or eight of them every day. I take the bus there after school and help her clean up her brushes and stuff, then I go home with my mother on the bus when she gets off work. She goes you're late for work but I go it's not my fault because it was my first day and I couldn't find the stupid place. I wish I could work at McDonalds. I think I'm old enough to sell frites if I'm old enough to XXX with boys ha ha –
    Chelle

~

Dear Mrs Legère:
Thank you very much for permitting your young daughter Rochelle to assist me whilst I am indisposed with my injured shoulder. I am sure she will learn her tasks before long.

Just between us, do you find she has trouble learning? At my age it is to be expected, but I wonder if she is perhaps just not accustomed to receiving and remembering instruction. I have no idea what they teach in school these days. Of course, in my day, it was all about memorization, and respect for your elders. Things were stricter for us overseas than here.

No matter. I do appreciate that Rochelle was willing to try to help me. She has informed me that 'minimum wage' is now $9 per hour, even for unskilled, untrained, under-age children? This seems extraordinarily dear to me, but I have enclosed $27 to pay for the three hours she has worked this past week.

If I have over-paid, it can be applied toward next week's wages.
Sincerely,
B. Hilchey

~

Dearest Mae -
Whatever shall I do? The young girl who is coming to "help" me in the studio is the worst possible! I do

not exaggerate! She is sullen and unresponsive—unless you call a shrug of the shoulders a response. I do not. I call it rude and I told her so in no uncertain terms!

I didn't ask her age, but she is much younger than all the make-up and jewellery she wears would lead one to believe. I had seen her only at a distance, and she seemed a mature teen-ager, I thought perhaps in High School, esp. with all those boys who follow in her wake. Up close she is a mere child, perhaps fourteen, but wears the make-up of Cleopatra or worse, I daren't say what. This is the truth!

I haven't mentioned this to the mother, who, for reasons I would rather not know, is raising the child on her own. But even a child should be able to pay attention and understand that PAINTS ARE EXPENSIVE! I watch her for mistakes, so her wastefulness won't be repeated.

When I think of how responsible you and I were in our early teens! Earlier!

My arm is no better yet, but the young "Dr" says it is healing and I am to leave it alone, and surely he knows best!

It's too bad it takes so long to hear from your tests but we just have to wait, don't we, no need to fret. Love you. Miss you.

Hugs (if I could),
Bella

~

Dear Mrs Hilchey

I sorry you accident your arm. Many order for your special hand-painted vase now and plate, price good, not so good to keep customer waiting. Try keep same shipment.

Mr. Fong

~

From: Rochelle Legere (bellechelle@notmail.com)
To: Celine Gaultier (lineisfine@noodle.com)
Subject: ugh!!!

Hi Line: I wish I was old enough to work somewhere at a real job. This old lady is real cranky. Do you remember M. Boismartin, our home room teacher? Well she's way worse. She told me to clean her brushes and throw away her paints and so I did and then she yelled at me but I don't know what for. I pack the dishes she paints into a boite to send to Montreal – I wished I could go in it to see you!!! And she yelled at me again cause I didn't press hard enuf on the label you stick on the top of the box. I'll be glad when I don't have to come to work for her.

– Your belle Chelle

~

Hello Reverend MacLean? This is Mrs. Hilchey calling, Bella Hilchey, you know, from your congregation at Saint Anselm's. I'm calling to explain why I haven't been able to attend services recently. I've had a slight accident at home – nothing very serious though it is very uncomfortable and I am unable to dress for church, as I am all alone. No need to visit me though. The young doctors say I must rest when I can until I am fully recovered and you know I must follow doctor's orders, much as I would prefer to come to your services. Until then, I am in great need of an assistant at my work for one hour, three days a week, which should suit a school student. I wondered, that is, the other reason I am calling is I wondered if you would be able to recommend one of the children in Saint Andrews' Sunday School, perhaps? It is important that the child be polite and able to take instruction. Please ring me if you have any suitable candidates for this position. It would mean so much to me. God bless you for all that you do. Bye-bye, now.

~

Dear Mrs Hilchey

Many damage in shipment. Two vase break and four plate crack or chip. No good pack in box. Broken and damage work no good, cannot sell, cannot pay for. Glass vase very special, price go up. Cost of six damage must deduct from pay. Please no more break! Pack good.

Mr. Fong

~

Dearest Mae –

I am so despondent. I can't do anything for myself, my shoulder is so sore and I find it so hard to do even simple things with my arm strapped so tightly to my body. I've had to ask that nasty superintendent in the building to open Puss' food cans. I mustn't even take off the bandage to wash! "Dr" says it will heal better that way and I am not to cut the bandages under any circumstances! I wonder how he would feel if it happened to him? Young people just don't understand what we have gone through in our lives, and how much we appreciate AND DESERVE a little consideration.

To make matters worse, that child who comes to 'help' me at my studio has cost me <u>a lot</u> of money. I asked her to pack my week's work in the shipping carton to return it to Montreal, and seal it and write the label for it. I had to remind her to press <u>HARD</u> on the mailing form as she was making three copies. Do they teach these children nothing in the schools today?

Well, Mae dear, today I received a stern note from Mr Fong telling me that six pieces had broken in transit! I was mortified! Sure enough, I searched my studio and there was all the packing material that should have been in the box between the pieces - still in the cupboard! And I am out a lot of money. I don't suppose I will be able to withhold the girl's pay, as it's all about the employee these days, not the hard-working employer. Not like when we first went into service in dirty old Glasgow, is it, Mae? Those were hard days, but I think then young people knew their place!

I was disappointed that Mr Fong would imply I was not doing a good job, too. My flower-vases are very popular, and he never says thank-you, just "paint many quick". Sometimes I think I should try to find another wholesaler for my talents.

Don't fuss about your test results, Mae. Do you think they really know about these things? They are all so young, these "Drs". I'm sure when you meet with your old family physician that he will have some medicine for you to take to make it all better.

Much love from your suffering sister, Bella

~

From: Rochelle Legere (bellechelle@notmail.com)
To: Celine Gaultier (lineisfine@noodle.com)
Subject: help me

This job SUCKS!!! The box of stuff I packed up to ship to Montreal got dropped or something and some of her vozzes got broke and she blamed me! I was so mad when she was yelling I just sat and wouldn't talk. She went on and on about packing but she never told me how to do it before I sent them, all she cared about was how hard I pressed on the label. She said she wanted to take the losses from my wages, but I haven't earned enough. Can you believe each one of her vozzes sells for over $100? She does six a day. That's easy money. Wish I could do that. She can afford to lose a few.

Since we came here I only speak francais at home or in French class at school, but when Missus Hilchee was yelling at me I swore at her en francais, and you know what she does? She looks right at me and goes you should be ashamed of yourself. En francais! Blew me away! She didn't say anything else so I guess I'm not busted. Maman makes me pay if I swear, like I'm a baby!

'Chelle

~

Dear Mr Fong:

As I told you I injured my arm so have had to take on a very inexperienced girl to help me, and it was she who failed to use the packing material in the last shipment.

I am very sorry that some of the vases/plates were broken upon arrival, but I don't think that I should be penalized for the loss of the raw material. My artwork is very popular and worth a lot more than those imported vases I paint on – which I do feel are not up to the quality of former years.

I believe the shipper insures the contents so you should apply for recompense from them. If I must lose the compensation for my flowers, so be it, but I do not accept that I should pay you for the glass. I have often thought those cartons were inadequate for such fragile contents. Perhaps you could find something sturdier?

Also, if you would be so kind, please ensure that the vases are cleaned before you ship them to me. They are coated in some sort of oily dust when they arrive and I find it very difficult and a waste of my studio time to clean them prior to painting on them. I don't recall receiving them in such a condition in years gone by.

Quality does matter, Mr Fong, and that goes for everyone.

Yours truly,
B. Hilchey

~

Dear Mae:
This child is a case! (Her name is Rochelle). Her family are francophone, from Montreal, as I discovered when she swore at me in French the other day, the rude little snippet, thinking I wouldn't know what filth she had uttered! Well I looked right at her and said – in French – that she should be ashamed of herself! That set her back on her heels.

It's obvious there is no father-figure in her family. Can you imagine if we had sassed Father? We would have been taking our tea standing up for a very long time! Well I remember! Perhaps you don't, dear, as you were always his favourite. It wasn't pleasant, but look how we turned out. I don't expect as much for this child.

She will not pay attention to my instructions. I tried to explain things slowly and clearly, but all she did was roll her eyes and shrug. She asked me where I was from, and I said, still proud as anything after all these years abroad, that I was frae Edinburgh in dear old Scotland. She then asked me where that was, which was a refreshing display of curiosity on her part, if not intelligence. I informed her Scotland was in the UK. Then she asked me what language they speak there! I wonder why they pay those teachers so much if they don't teach basic geography in schools today!

My shoulder is very itchy, which "Dr" says is a sign that it is healing, though I sincerely doubt that. I think there was more he could have done besides wrap it up in tape, in this day and age. I do hope I shan't be crippled for the rest of my life. Drat that Puss! He stays well away from my feet now, I can tell you.

Mae, dear, I think you should see if there isn't another doctor you could consult regarding your troubles, a specialist in Edinburgh, maybe? To undergo surgery on just one physician's say-so seems risky. However, they can do wonders these days, if they have a mind to.

Much love as ever,

Bella

~

From: Rochelle Legere (bellechelle@notmail.com)
To: Celine Gaultier (lineisfine@noodle.com)
Subject: Weird!

You know what? Elle parle francais! I mean, like anyone in Montreal, not french from friggin' France like
they teach in school here. Like she lived there. Which
she said she did, back before the war, whatever that
means, not the war my Papa was killed in. She says it
with a number, like maybe the 1812 War, but I don't
know when that was. We haven't had that in school
yet, have you? I can't understand anything she says
in the kind of English they speak in Yookay where
she's from, wherever that is. But she talks like crazy
in French. And she's a lot nicer en francais, aussi.
Goes on and on about les rues downtown and makes
me homesick. Finally I'm like I have to go 'cause Maman is waiting for me but she was telling some long
story about going to a concert in Montreal and having to walk home across the city because she
couldn't afford the bus. Weird!
– Chelle

~

Hello Reverend MacDonald this is Bella Hilchey
calling you again, just in case you hadn't received my
message the first time, you know how these gadgets
are, never sure of them, nothing like talking face-to-
face, is there? I was hoping you could find a polite
young person at Saint Avard's to assist me whilst I
am indisposed due to a somewhat serious injury. I
should think that parents today would want to have
their children assist their elders in need in the congregation. Please do ring me as soon as you have the

names of some good and responsible youngsters I could interview. Thank-you and may God bless you, Reverend. Bye-bye, now.

~

Dearest Mae:
You recall I told you in my last letter that I had spoken in French to this teen-age girl who is supposedly helping me at my studio. Well, the strangest thing is that the French language—which I have not had call to speak since leaving "la belle province" to come to this old "New Scotland" city so many years ago—it's all coming back to me, and memories of places and things I have not thought of in such a very long time, too! Her family is from Montreal, too, near where my Charlie and I lived, though it is so different in that neighbourhood now. I told her what we used to do 'way back when', and do you know, she <u>paid attention</u> and <u>listened</u> to me. When she speaks in French, she is rather more well-spoken than in English, I am pleased to discover.

My letter is a short one today, dear, as I must go see "Dr" who will cut off these awful bandages and free my arm at last!

So sorry to hear you are feeling poorly after your little operation. There are some nasty bugs going 'round this time of year, perhaps you have caught one.

"Feed a cold and starve a fever" was always the 'medicine' we were given as children, wasn't it, so

follow that age-old advice for whichever you have—
though I never liked the "starve" treatment!
    Much love,
    Bella

~

From: Rochelle Legere (bellechelle@notmail.com)
To: Celine Gaultier (lineisfine@noodle.com)
Subject: I'm an artist!!!

'Line, guess what!! I'm an artist! No, really I am! I
painted something today for the old lady I work for
and she goes you did 'veddy weel', which she says is
English for tres bon, but I don't know her kind of
English or whatever.
    When she is nearly finished painting her flowers
on vozzes for the day, I'm supposed to clean her
brushes. She yelled at me last week for wasting
paint, so I asked her if she was sure she wanted me
to wipe off one brush that had a lot of paint still on
it. She said certainement and then goes no, wait,
here, watch this. She took out a plate and wiped the
brush on it and no word of a lie 'Line, it looked just
like a green leaf, like really. I'm like Wow can I do
that and she goes regardez and she put more paint
on the brush and painted a couple more leafs, and
then she gave me the brush and said Do it just like
that, and then she let me do it. I was sooooo scared,
but I did it just like she did and then we looked and
there were a whole bunch of leafs and mine looked

just as good as hers! That's when she said I did veddy weel! She smiled too, which made me remember my grand-maman.

She didn't say anything else about it but I think she thought I did ok. I can't stop thinking about it. Tomorrow I'm going to watch her make the rest of the pictures and see if I can copy what she does. It can't be that hard.

– Belle'Chelle

~

Dearest Mae:

What a disappointment! My arm is out of that awful binding but it is still so sore, and it has wasted away from disuse! I was <u>very</u> glad to be able to wash it, finally, with some mild Castile soap, and not a moment too soon, though I had to be gentle on the tender skin. And now my left arm can join me properly in my clothing, though it is not easy to do, let me tell you, as I cannot lift it very high yet.

The "Dr" has given me such unreasonable exercises to strengthen it, and I said to him that I wouldn't have needed the exercises had he but permitted me to move my arm all along, but he just laughed and said perhaps I was right, but just humour him. I'd like to bean him, is what I'd like to do! And when I'm out and about I'm to put it in a nasty sling around my neck, so I'm still an invalid.

That teenager girl has shown more interest in her work of late. I find if I instruct her <u>en français</u> she pays better attention. She insisted on trying out my paints as she was cleaning up today, and against my better judgment I allowed her to make a few strokes with a brush on an imperfect plate. She seemed to want to go on doing that so I had to remind her that she was there to work and clean brushes, not to waste expensive paints.

I find it odd, Mae, that I have not heard one peep from the Reverend at the local Presbyterian church, Saint Arthur's I think it is, whom I called to ask for the names of some other youngsters I might hire. One never gets to talk to him in person, of course, just that impersonal machine, recording everything one says and no way to do it over. Perhaps he has forgotten about old widowed Mrs Hilchey, do you suppose? They do that when you don't send $$ every month to remind them who you are. A shame. Father used to tithe, remember that? He supported the church enough for all of us, don't you agree? Even unto death.

I wouldn't put too much stock in what the specialists say, dear Mae. Sometimes I think they just study their "x-rays" in their dark rooms and forget all about the patient!

You have always been healthy, perhaps a bit heavy but that's our inheritance isn't it dear— look at Mother and her sisters—and they would know that if they came to see you instead of looking at their test results.

Perhaps you have a 'flu that has made the "x-rays" cloudy, as tuberculosis did for so many. Maybe you'd ask for them to be done over once you are feeling better. We must take control for ourselves, mustn't we?

All my love as always,
Bella

~

Dear Mrs Legere:
Yesterday your daughter Rochelle asked if she could use some of my paints to do a little painting of her own. Of course, paints are very dear and as she has had no instruction in art of any kind as far as I can tell, even after all those years in public school, I should be obliged to at least watch over her so that she does not destroy my brushes or waste paint. Perhaps I may give her the simplest of instruction, in the interests of self-preservation, as it were.

If it is your wish that she be permitted to engage in this activity at my studio, I should think it fair if I were to pay her only for the part of the hour she actually works for me, and not for the time she plays at her own project. I will not charge for my instruction at this time.

Of course, this will be only as work permits, as I unfortunately still require assistance to package my items for shipment and clean up etc.

If you are in agreement with this, please send along a note with Rochelle when she next comes to my studio.

B. Hilchey

~

From: Rochelle Legere (bellechelle@notmail.com)
To: Celine Gaultier (lineisfine@noodle.com)
Subject: je suis artiste

Dear Celine: I'm a painter!!! The old lady—Mrs Hil-chee—is showing me how to paint more leafs and other stuff for backgrounds on her plates and vozzes. She yells at me if I make the slightest mistake, but I don't care because I just love to do it and I want to learn to do it right. She doesn't want to pay me while I'm painting and she won't show me anything if there is any cleaning up left to do for her so I have to work faster and today I got an early bus downtown so I could have more time to paint. Maybe someday I will be a great artist and have an exhibition at a gallery in Montreal LOL! That would be fantastic! You would come—no, you would be the gallery owner and lots of very rich men would come to see us!!! Would I sign my name Rochelle or just 'Chelle, I think 'Chelle what do you think?
  - Chelle

~

Ma chère Mme Hilchey
  You are very kind to employ my daughter and she is very much enjoying her time with you in your art studio. She is a smart girl and I am trying to teach

her to be independent and responsible, which has not been easy for her or for me since her father was killed overseas in military service for our country.

I will leave the financial arrangement to work out between you. If she prefers to use some of her time with you to learn to paint and you are satisfied with that, so be it.

Merçi beaucoup,
Manon Legere

~

Dear Mae:

It seems I shan't be able to be free of this child who has been 'helping' me. I felt my arm was sufficiently healed that I could take over the work myself —must watch expenses, you know—but at the end of my first day on my own I was <u>so</u> tired. I intended to soldier on, of course, as we were taught, but on Thursday, in she pops as though she were invited—but she hadn't come to work for me and I made it clear I would not pay her unless I asked her to come.

No, she came to ask me if she could use my paints and my plates for a school project! Such audacity! It is evident that they do not teach children in school anything about art, especially not the ancient Oriental style for which I am known.

Imagine, after all the years of training and experience I have, she points to a very valuable plate I had begun working on and says can she "do one" for a school project!! Just like that, a Rembrandt in our midst!

I'm certain she doesn't have the wherewithal to pay for materials, let alone for instruction. I understand her late father was in the military, she never speaks of him. I bargained with her to resume her work for me for 45 minutes in return for 15 minutes of painting, and we'd call it square.

Do you know what she said to that very generous offer, Mae? She said "OK"! Not thank-you ever so much for your generosity, no no. But we shall see.

I'm so glad you have someone coming in to help you too, dear Mae, until you recover from this episode. I wonder why your "Dr" refused to operate again? Perhaps you need some extra vitamins, especially if you can't keep your food down as you say, poor thing. There are so many supplements at the chemists, and someone there could tell you which ones would be best for you. They do here, they come right out from behind their counters and can't help you enough. I take what they recommend and am feeling very well, except for my poor shoulder. I don't tell "Dr" what meds I take, as he says he doesn't care for them. Probably doesn't know what they are.

From your loving sister,
Bella

~

From: Rochelle Legere (bellechelle@notmail.com)
To: Celine Gaultier (lineisfine@noodle.com)
Subject: Cinque Foil

Hey 'Line - Do you know what is cinque foil? It's called a Wild Rose here, a flower that grows on bushes all over the place, and I'm painting one for my school project. Missus Hilchee thinks it's an art project but it's not it's for science class. Mister Dyer told us we had to learn all about one plant and bring in a representation of it, and he means make one, not pick one. So I'm studying the Wild Rose and Missus H is showing me how to make the leafs and stem and thorns this week. She won't let me paint them on the plate until I practice on paper and get it perfect but I am practising at home too so I think I will get it vite. I get to paint it on the plate on Friday and I'm soooo nervous. I don't have any paints at home but I took home a brush that she told me to throw away—honest, I didn't steal it, I asked her if I could have it—and I just practise the strokes with a dry brush and close my eyes and pretend that I am doing it. I just love it, 'Line! I want to be a great artist someday!

She says next week we'll work on the petals and then there's yellow stuff in the centre—pistils and stamens, I have to write about what every part is for class so I learned that.

Maybe you'll call your art gallery the Cinque Foil! We'll be known as the two Wild Roses! We'll wear high heels and lots of MAKEUP!!!

–'Chelle

~

Dearest Mae:

I know you haven't been able to write while you're feeling so poorly, but I do miss your letters so, and look forward to receiving them again soon. Perhaps you could get one of the helpers who come in to make your tea to write me a little note telling me how you are.

I am very pleased to inform you that my protégé, Rochelle, has received top honours in her school's art project with a charming little wild rose she painted on a small tea plate—with my instruction, of course. The whole thing was a rush job, as she didn't inform me of her desire to do this until only a few days before the project was due. But we persevered and though her work is very amateurish, as you would expect, it was quite good for the effort. I think she might have some talent, and I have spoken to her mother about it.

Perhaps next autumn when she enters High School she will apprentice with me. I have often thought how wonderful it would be to pass on my art to someone—not that I intend to retire. We'll go on forever, won't we, Mae dear, just like Father did, nearly a century of strict living, which a small flock of sheep will do for you. Poor Mother was not so lucky, was she, with that horrid cancer taking her so much earlier, though she did well to last as long as she did. You were such a comfort to her, though what could you do?

My shoulder is progressing, though it still has twinges when I put up my hair, but at least I can leave that awful sling at home now. I still have Rochelle to assist me with the boxes, and she has restored some of my favourite brushes that I had feared were lost, so she is turning out to be of some use. I would not want to repeat that Winter again, and I have told Puss to never trip me again <u>or else</u>!

Please don't stop writing to me, Mae, even though you don't much feel like it, as I do so enjoy your notes. Father used to say that we should do something we don't like to do each day, and I know I follow his example in that. I think writing to me must do you good, helps you focus on something else besides your discomforts. I assure you I read every word.

Much love, your only sister,
Bella

~

Mrs Legere

I am writing this in haste as the taxicab has been called to take me to the airport. Thank-you very much for permitting Rochelle to tend my old cat whilst I am in Scotland with my sister, who has been ailing for some time.

When her nurse rang me up I thought I could not go all the way over there just to cheer her—after the winter I have had—but they seemed to think it would help her and so I shall. After all, she's the only family I have left on either side of the Ocean.

I know Rochelle is young and wanting to be outside with her young friends these spring days, but Puss will be happier if she spends a little time with him each day. To help her pass the time I have brought a few brushes and some paints home from the studio for her to use if she wishes – in the kitchen only, please, <u>not</u> in my sitting-room.

I have left some newspapers for her to spread to catch drips. Mr Fong sent an imperfect vase (happens too often!) so I have left that for her to paint on. She has been trying to imitate my lovely old fashioned flowers and I thought she might like to try one on a vase of her own.

Perhaps you will like to keep the finished product in your home when she has completed it. My professionally-painted ones fetch a high price.

I should return within a week or ten days.

B. Hilchey

PS If you would be so kind, I would be less uneasy about this arrangement if you would personally ensure that Rochelle has locked my door each day and returned the key to your care. I'm sure you understand. She is very young.

Thank-you. BH

~

Dear Mrs Hilchey

Got message you go away. Box already ship, no lose please. Many orders, customer calling where is my flower-vase from China-painter? Please not long to delay. Mr Fong

~

From: Rochelle Legere (bellechelle@notmail.com)
To: Celine Gaultier (lineisfine@noodle.com)
Subject: on my own

Dear Celine:

It's the best!! Mrs Hilchee had to fly to the Yookay to look after her sister and left me with the key to her apartment, which is just up the street from our place. I have to feed her old cat and scoop his poop (yuck!) but all he does is sleep anyway. But guess what!! She left me a whole bunch of paints and brushes and one of her precious vozzes to paint on while she is away! I'm in heaven! I'm not allowed to bring anyone up here = NO BOYS!! LOL That's OK 'cause I really want to have a nice voz painted when she comes back so she will teach me more. It's still just flowers but I like them. My mother gave me some glass bottles to practice on so I won't ruin the voz. Wish you could see it.

'Chelle, your artist friend

~

From: Rochelle Legere (bellechelle@notmail.com)
To: Celine Gaultier (lineisfine@noodle.com)
Subject: merde!

Hi 'Line:

I'm glad old Mrs Hilchee is away! I was painting on her kitchen table yesterday and forgot to put the newspapers out like she said to and her old cat woke up and tried to jump up on the table and nearly knocked over the voz! I caught it before it fell—grace a dieu!!—but I dropped my brush and he stepped on that and ran with paint on his foot and I yelled and he spread it everywhere!!! Thank goodness I have lots and lots of experience in cleaning up paints, but still I didn't know if I found it all or not as that old cat ran and hid after I started yelling at him! Like she will yell at me if she sees one tiny drop of paint on anything!!! He didn't come out the rest of the day but he showed up to eat today.

But after I cleaned up I found some paint splatters on a little wine glass she had left in the sink, and the paint was stuck on good—it's special waterproof paint supposed to stay on glass, so that's why. I thought I was in deep merde but then I thought I would just make her a painting on it as a surprise, so I thought about it and then I made it. You should see it, 'Line. The whole wine glass is a flower, like a tulip. The stem is the stem and the bowl is the petals and leafs. It's really pretty. I took it home to show Maman and she nearly cried, it was that good. She said my Papa would have been so proud of me and that made me feel très bon.

I hope Mrs Hilchee likes it. You never know about her, but I am learning not to listen when she yells. She knows how to paint, that's for sure.

I love going to Missus Hilchee's place after school.

I pretend it's my own apartment, and that I go down the street just to visit my Maman. Will you and me have our own apartment above the Cinque Foil Gallery? You can sell my paintings downstairs and I will paint more upstairs! Can't wait!!!

'Chelle

~

Dear Mr Fong:

I am writing to advise you that I have returned home to Canada, rather later than I had anticipated due to the unexpected death of my sister, my last remaining relative, while I was overseas. The loss has created a great hardship for me, as I was forced to spend several weeks taking care of her final affairs in Scotland before returning to my own work here.

I find I am exhausted and must rest awhile before resuming regular production. I will inform you of when that will be.

On a more positive note, I have acquired an apprentice, a young artist, originally from Montreal, who I understand has some good connections there with a potential gallery. Once I am back on my feet, I expect my apprentice will be able to assist me—and you—in supplying customers with the quantity and quality of hand-painted vases and plates they desire.

Mlle Leger, my apprentice, is also developing a line of new floral goblet items which we may offer you, but more about that later.

Thank-you for your understanding during this

most difficult time for me.
    Sincerely,
    Bella Hilchey

Suite 102: The Wordist Again

Welcome back, everyone. That was a refreshing break, wasn't it? Even with the light pollution here on the waterfront we were able to spy quite a few stars on this chilly night before the fire department finally gave the "all clear".

Thanks to those of you who have returned to hear the remainder of my address, though I'm sorry that Her Honour had to call it a night.

Now, if you recall, I was about to describe my fellow tenants in the old building in which I had my writing studio, as potential characters in future stories.

One office was occupied by a lady who did some sort of counselling. I met her one day when our shared newspaper, left on the floor-model ashtray by the elevator, was folded open to a report of a serious house fire in a village in the county. There was a big photo of a firefighter carrying a young woman down a ladder from her bedroom window, a very dramatic scene. The photographer had caught the young volunteer's face, which was all grin, framed by thick smoke and flames. The counsellor lady saw the photo and cried for joy. We all came out of our offices that time to see what the commotion was about. She wouldn't explain her connection with the story, but her tears in place of her usual reserve touched us all.

In another office, a pugnacious private eye interviewed suspects, I deduced, whom very large policemen and policewomen escorted in. While I sometimes wanted to tell *him* to tone it down, I'd get a heavy thump on the wall between our offices if I was trying out dialogue while he was roasting a suspect on the grill. I felt secure when he was around, even though he was the reason many undesirables came into the building. I doubted they would return on their own, and if they tried they would not likely find our obscure front door.

Like that private eye, I, too, seek 'persons of interest'. Our readers demand that we wordists make our cops and robbers far more interesting than real ones. Reality is either dull or crazy-weird; that's why you turn to stories. Fiction has to be steadily exciting yet oh, so credible. Wordists must re-order the order of things for your entertainment without showing you our fingerprints on it.

Nobody expects music to be better than itself.

The office with which I shared my other wall was the studio of a painter, an elderly Scottish lady who was very prim and proper. I was verbalising a steamy romance scene one day as she passed by my door. She said loudly in her Scots brogue that "the profaesional office is nooo place for such goings-on."

Notice how I said 'prim and proper' just now? If writing a story I would have to discard either 'prim' or 'proper' or find another descriptor altogether, as those two words together are a hackneyed phrase and readers would say I was not original if I used it. In music, you love to sing the same old choruses over and over, arms over shoulders, stumbling to recall the words and laughing when you get them wrong. In writing, readers want every sentence to be as fresh as the first lines of Genesis, and you know Who was the author of that book. Wordists, from Him on down, must be ever original.

Speaking of God, a kindly old minister of some stripe came to his little office across the hall once or twice a week to sell sermons to those less gifted in that task—a writing gig I wouldn't mind having myself. He would tap on my door before meeting with his clients and ask me about myself, how the writing was going, et cetera. He was such a good listener. I was quite fond of him, though I learned little about him. I was always quiet while he was in, though he never asked me to be.

Wordists are suckers for listeners, as you might well imagine. We would—and do—starve for an attentive audience. In fact, most wordists are psychologically and clinically needy in our desire to be heard or read. Listeners are the caterpillar in the cocoon; readers are the metamorphosed Luna moths who will dance 'round our published flame, should that happen in our lifetime.

There are two main categories of writing: fiction and non-fiction. I struggle with this bifurcation. I mean, can you leave what is and enter what is not, and how, and how would you know? It reminds me of the salesman demonstrating vacuum flasks that would keep hot drinks hot and cold drinks cold: someone in the audience asked, "How does it know?"

Music doesn't have music and non-music. It has rests, very precise ones, indicating silence, which is a higher form of music. Non-music is noise, as journalism is to writing. Echoes are about architecture, not music, a product of what the music is *in*, but in writing we must know what the echo is *of.*

Here's a specific application of this important point, as it may apply to a whodunit. And by the way, all stories are whodunits. Without a question to start with, the story is as flat as the earth once was. I say that because "flat as a pancake" is over-used and as a practitioner of the wordist's art I feel obliged to reach past the low-hanging fruit. More established authors like your Hemingways and your Atwoods can lard their books with 'flat as a pancake' on every page and who would dare protest, but I haven't attained their impunity.

Back to whodunits. A specific application of the 'this vs non-this' concept is in the words 'guilty' and 'innocent', the very essence of whodunits. These words give a perfect case-study of dead ends and loose ends. You see, one must be guilty *of* something, or at least accused of something. Guilty of murder, of theft, of snitching, of impure thoughts. *Guilty as sin* is not good enough. One must be more specific than suspicious.

That's as hard to do as it is to say.

It is often said that he who is not guilty is innocent.

But oh, my friends, we must not stop there. "Innocent" is a lonely, dimly-lit bus stop in a bad part of town where the last bus is always late. Move away from there quickly before someone gets hurt, or before a pool of blood is discovered, just beyond the pool of light, with foot-prints in it that match your shoes.

The law says we are innocent *until proven guilty*. That potential is a very heavy metal lining in your whodunit cloud.

My preferred hierarchy is that babies are born innocent—*of* everything, not just sin. As we grow older we are still innocent—*of* many things—and when we die we may be innocent still—*of* some things.

If a story states that the non-guilty is simply innocent, there remains no story to write. A dead end. A great story explores what people are innocent *of*, or not. Loose ends all over the place.

In other words, guilty is about what you is, not what you ain't. You may lose a great story if you don't follow that little two-letter clue spelled o-f. I call it the "Wizard of Of". Thank you. You are too kind.

Beg pardon? Your crème brulée has been repaired...no? Lemon pie now, is it? So quickly!

So to conclude, then: my fellow tenants and I would meet occasionally on the fire escape at the back of the building for a break from our toils if the weather and harbourside aromas were tolerable.

We gathered there the day we each found an eviction notice from the landlord under our doors. He had sold the building to be developed into an eco-urban organic hydroponic farm co-op with solar panels and goats on a sod roof. You may have heard about it.

It's under appeal, of course. People who never knew the old building existed are now fighting to preserve its heritage. The developers argue that it was never a building *per se*, but a roofed-over alleyway between buildings, so it never really existed, in fact or in fiction. I favour the latter theory myself.

We appointed the private eye to check out other locations for us. He found a building on Almon Street in the north end of the city, with warehouse spaces in its centre and offices around the perimeter, or maybe it was the other way around. It was vacant, a century newer, and the entrance was nondescript.

The old reverend said it sounded like the promised land. The painter said her business was expanding and she needed a larger studio at ground level for easier shipping, so this sounded good for her. We wondered if the over-decorated teenager who worked with her might attract the wrong sort of clientele to the building, but the old lady said firmly, "The gairrl comes wi' me," sounding just like one of my characters might if I had time to work out how to write her brogue. The counsellor said it was a dream come true. The private eye had already spied his office in the place.

There was also an unofficial tenant. Al had picked up coffees and muffins for us, things that we who are desk-bound need to keep ourselves awake and working, especially me. We'd leave our orders for Al under the glass dish in the giant ashtray by the elevator—an ashtray that hadn't been used for years, of course, but which nobody felt the need to discard. All agreed that we should invite Al to similarly haunt the new site. The reverend offered to ask Al to transport the ashtray to the new place as it had served us all so well, and neither the preservationists nor the urban farmers were likely to treasure it as we did.

But, the private eye reported, there was one hitch. There were five of us tenants on Barrington Street, and only four offices on Almon, and he knew of no other suitable space available in a 'decent' part of the city. By 'decent', he explained, he meant an area where you weren't likely to be dodging bullets, but I don't know if that describes any part of the city now.

So we each filled out secret ballots for the three tenants we'd like to share the new space with.

I received the least number of votes.

And so, even though I have told you the story of these folk, I cannot tell you what became of them.

Or of me either. A dead end.

Thank you.

The Sub-basement

He had acquired the knack of being invisible, un-detectable, indiscernible. He could hide in a shadow, or be a shadow, a dark patch of bark on a tree, a ripple in a stream.

This skill would have been highly valued in espionage, but he knew he wouldn't last a moment in that game. Fear would light him up in the darkest night and expose him to snipers skilled in looking for shadows. His abiding desire was to safeguard the life of one man—himself.

Over many long months of hiding where people didn't look or recognize what they saw, he had time to debate with his conscience. If he carried on being invisible, he would live. If he joined any side, he'd have to kill, or others would die protecting him, and then he would die anyway.

The war ended. Invisibility had served him in wartime, and he hoped it would lead him to a good life in peacetime. When he allowed himself to speak with someone, it was to offer to work in tucked-away places.

He was small, not muscular, but wiry. He could fit into spaces inaccessible to most labourers and machines, climbing down wells or scaling buildings without a ladder. He would take whatever coin was offered for his service and be gone.

He eventually made his way to a seaport where ships were transporting displaced persons to Canada for a new life. Men were sought to work in Canada for good pay. They were giving away land in Canada. The Canadian government encouraged families to settle and have many children.

Soon he learned which types of vessels offered the best comfort and safety across the stormy North Atlantic Ocean. He fled from one ship, its gleaming white paint and tidy decks affording no hiding place. He waited and watched. When a rusty converted freighter came alongside and put out its gangplank for human cargo, he knew it was the rainbow that would carry him to the new world.

He had sometimes stolen food or clothing, but only to survive and never from those who had less than he. His rucksack contained a collection of hats acquired in his travels. In a crowd of people jostling shoulder to shoulder, hats indicated that this one's a farmer, over there's a miner, that one's a gentleman, here's a labourer. His hats blended him into the crowd when he couldn't hide.

A man had set a suitcase down on the quay. With split-second timing, he picked it up and hastily carried it up the gangway, following close behind a woman who was struggling with her little children, as though he was her porter, wearing a porter's hat as he was. A hullabaloo arose on the dock about stolen baggage, but the suitcase was soon located unharmed on the ship's deck. The porter had disappeared, and the woman he had followed remained unaware of the entire event.

The voyage was slow, rough, and cold enough to threaten the life of the small stowaway. He spent a good deal of time on deck amongst the jumble of rusty cables and damage from enemy artillery or storms. He spent some very cold nights in the bottom of a wooden lifeboat swinging from the davits, but the ocean winds blew salt spray through the gaps in the strakes, so he chose as often as possible to hide in the warm engine room despite the deafening engine racket and slopping, poisonous bilge water.

When the ship finally docked at Halifax, he knew immigration would ask to see his documents, and he had none. He remained on board and watched the crew. They were planning unauthorized shore leave that night. One by one, they crept along to the foredeck, where the heavy hawsers held the ship to the bollards on the pier. Hand-over-hand, they swung across the gap and soon were gone into the old city, shadows themselves, no alarm raised.

When they were out of sight he followed suit, pulling himself across and onto the dock.

From a safe distance, he followed the crew. They were in high spirits, and appeared to be heading to a familiar destination. It was by now closer to dawn than sunset, but they stopped at a building where lights shone in all the windows and through an open door, which they entered. The crew had sailors' traditional business on their minds, and they would do it with vigour and haste before returning to the ship.

He did not join them, nor return to the ship. He was going to find his new home on dry land, in this war-free country.

A few streets farther along were office buildings. In an alley between two buildings, he spied a door propped open, leading into a low cellar. He cautiously approached the doorway and saw a bucket with a mop leaning against the wall in the small space. There was a large sink and a cold water tap nearby. He lifted the bucket to the tap and ran the water into it. He began to mop the floor, and finally allowed himself to be seen.

From that day on, he worked for the telephone company.

His name was Zoltan Zabç, or something like that. Nobody wrote or pronounced his name correctly. He had rarely spoken it himself in his young life. Zabich, his boss said, you do a good job at this and you'll have steady work. Just use these—he pointed to the mops and soaps and de-greasers and such—and clean up whatever lands down here.

At first glance, the job didn't look full-time, but then his bulky boss lifted an iron bar on a metal door and showed him a low-ceilinged area weakly illuminated with one light bulb. When the elevator came to rest at basement Level B, over their heads, the cables and hoses beneath the car dangled into this pit, along with gobs of grease and an assortment of small objects that fell into the gap between the car and the thresholds of the floors above.

Over time, those objects might get caught up and interfere with the elevator's smooth operation, so they needed cleaning up regularly. To do so, a man had to step over the barrier around the pit and down into the greasy bottom—and climb out again. The boss was of a size and condition that made this manoeuvre unsafe for him.

If the elevator was called to the basement, a man caught in the pit might have to lie down in the sludge to avoid being crushed, and wait for the elevator to be called to a higher floor. Which could be the next day, or after the weekend.

You'll have no trouble doing that, Zabich, the boss said. You're small and nimble. Just don't get fat.

With some of his meagre pay, he could afford to rent a small room with access to a toilet and cold water. He lined up occasionally at soup kitchens. He found clothes. He saved as much as he could from his weekly pay envelope, and eventually—weeks later—he had a tidy sum tucked away in the recesses of his domain beneath the building's basement floor.

Zabich had no way of knowing what this tidy sum was worth, if it would buy what he desired. He had food and shelter, but he dearly desired the company of a certain young woman.

He had seen her. She worked in another of the big stone buildings farther along the street. She, too, arrived for work early and left late, but hers was the night shift, on the opposite side of the clock to his.

Her clothes were threadbare, and she didn't wear boots, not even in the deepest snow or wettest slush.

He saw her step into the alleyway and remove the bags she wore over her cracked shoes before entering the side door to her workplace. He was in that alleyway, invisible, and saw her do it, saw her slender ankles, her graceful movements.

He also saw her face, and he thought she was most beautiful. He wanted to see more of her, to speak to her and hear her speak, see her smile. But how? He could bow and say hello to her, but what then? He chastised himself for neglecting to learn more than the necessary English words at work, mostly about grease and grime. In his rooming-house, there were no books of language instruction. No books at all, just a few tattered magazines, and he knew the language in those would not convey a chaste and respectful greeting.

There was a stone cathedral up the hill from his workplace. He had avoided going in there—he was ashamed of himself later to think of this—because he didn't want to give away the pennies he would've felt obliged to put in the box when he lit a candle, and why else would he go in there if not to light a candle?

From his cache, he now took one coin and some folding money. He pushed open the heavy sanctuary doors. He dropped the coin in the box and lit a candle for his family, so long ago and far away and gone. Then he entered the confessional and said the words through the grill that he had learned to say as a child.

Off the boats, are you, said the priest. Well, my son, I have no idea what sins you are confessing, but I'm sure you have committed all of the usual, so—

He pressed his money to the grill, and said *Tanul Ingles*. He recited the two dozen or so words he knew, and then repeated them. To his everlasting credit, the priest caught on. Those are all the words you know, son? You want to learn English? Wait here.

The priest who came out to see what he was jabbering about didn't know his mother tongue, but they knew enough languages between them that they could communicate at a basic level. He simply wanted to tell the young woman that he thought she was beautiful. Oh, yes, and to ask if he could buy her a coffee when she got off work some morning.

He ached to sit with her. He was so lonely. He hadn't been aware before, but now that he had seen her, he was lonely to the marrow in his bones.

He could express none of this in English, but when he spoke in his own tongue, his face translated it all perfectly. He again offered his money.

The priest glanced at his clothes, his hands darkened with grease, his dirty boots, and told him to keep his paper money, but to bring a coin for the box next time, each time. He would meet him here at the entrance to the church and teach him essential phrases, one each visit, until he was confident enough to approach the girl.

Never was there a keener student of language. Good morning, miss, please, what is your name, thank you, these were words in the language of love. May I see you again was a romantic opera. I will buy you coffee was an international treaty. He learned to say them and to understand her possible responses, and the priest praised his diligence.

He was soon ready to greet her, but he couldn't just jump out of the early-morning shadows without frightening her. He must offer her something, and this was not the season for flowers. He had seen the perfect gift in the window of a shop on the street above the basilica. It cost more than he'd ever spent on himself, but he didn't want to begin with her by offering a mere token.

At first, the clerk seemed reluctant to serve him in the shop, but he removed his cap, bowed deeply, smiled his best smile, and sweetly said please may I, as he had learned. The words were new, but he'd always had charm. He showed his money, and left with a box tied up with ribbon, carrying it in a kraft bag with handles.

The next morning, he scrubbed himself and nervously stood in plain sight under the streetlamp at the entrance to her alleyway.

She emerged at the end of her shift, leaned against the building as usual, pulled the plastic bread bags over her shoes before looking up, and there he stood and she was startled anyway.

Please, miss, may I take you for coffee? He'd blurted out the wrong words first.

She didn't respond, of course. He persisted for several mornings. She frowned at him and told him to go away. He couldn't win a glance, let alone a smile. He held out the kraft bag by the handles each time, but she would not acknowledge it.

Please, miss, what is your name?

She trudged away up the slushy street and he'd watch her go, taking his heart with her.

One day, he hid but didn't greet her. She came out as usual, appeared to look around for him, and seemed disappointed that he wasn't there. The next day, before she emerged from the side door in the alley, he placed the bag on the snow right outside the door, and stepped into the shadows.

Of course she recognized the carrier bag by now. She looked around for the smiling little man who'd been greeting her, but she didn't see him. Of course she was curious about him and what he'd been offering her. She grasped the handles, and quickly walked away with the bag.

His heart leaped with joy. Surely she would speak to him once she saw what he had given her.

She didn't emerge the next morning. He was almost late for the start of his own shift, waiting for her. Had she gone to work the night before? Was there another door? How could he know? Who could he ask?

Finally, two agonizing mornings later, she came out into the alley at the end of her shift as before, and he was waiting to greet her again. This time, she had plenty of questions. Where had he acquired the money for these boots? She was wearing them and they fit her perfectly and he smiled. Why had he given them to her? What did he want? Her father had accused her of stealing them, and he even asked at the store, where they told him they'd been purchased by a man whose description easily matched him.

He understood little of this speech. The priest's lessons had not provided him with words for this conversation. As she told him her story, he waited patiently, loving the sound of her voice, loving when she attempted to frown at him despite his obvious happiness, and he was overcome when she thanked him for his generosity.

He was emboldened then to ask her again if she would have coffee with him.

Yes, she would.

The light spilling out from the old café window became a happy beacon for them, and they sought its warm harbour as often as they could through that winter. She had a good ear for language, so they were soon sharing the words essential to fill up both their emptinesses. She took care to pronounce Zoltan Zabç correctly. She always called him by his full name, and he became himself at last.

He took her to show the priest the woman who had stolen his heart. They walked hand-in-hand up to the shoe store to thank them for making it possible for her to trust him.

The astute manager noted her slender ankles and sweet smile, and offered her a job on the spot. A day job, with better pay and a discount on shoes and boots.

Time passed.

He continued to serve in the sub-basement, though the dampness that seeped out of the bedrock and the fumes that sank to the lowest level of the building made his small body far less agile than it had once been.

Much had changed quickly in the world following the war. Most of it was over his head, literally and theoretically, but he continued to do a job that he could do well, that his boss appreciated, and he was left alone to do it. He was content.

One day, his boss came down to the small door, something he rarely did any more. He used to bring down the pay envelope containing cash every week. More recently, pay was deposited directly to the joint bank account his wife had set up for them.

When the boss crouched into the sub-basement, it wasn't to bring good news. The company was expanding, and soon the old building would be replaced by a modern office tower. Neither man was licensed to work on new elevators and escalators. His boss thanked him for his dedication to the go-nowhere job. They don't make 'em like you any more, Zabich. You're one of a kind. They shook hands.

He still came to work. Nobody had changed the lock on the low door. Perhaps he had the only key. The old elevator needed him to attend to its unseen needs until it was decommissioned. He knew its strengths and weaknesses, knew when to push and pull on its cables, how to keep its passengers safe.

Even after the electricity was disconnected and the elevator ceased to glide up and down its rails, he still came downtown to watch the construction through the hoarding. Seeing the new building absorb the old one was fascinating.

He knew enough about subterfuge to see that this expansion was dodging its way around regulations. As the new rose above the old, he saw that the corner housing the shaft of the elevator–*his* elevator–was now absorbed into a new structure on the side, created by roofing over the narrow alleyway.

Aside from being curious about what was happening, he had another motivation for coming to his old workplace: his pay had continued without interruption. There was even a small bonus tacked on at Christmas.

His wife was alarmed by this and they discussed it many times. They didn't argue: he had never disagreed with his beloved. He reassured her that he was kept on the payroll so that he would continue to look after the elevator pit, which he would do as soon as construction was completed.

He did think it odd that his pay continued without a message from any of the bosses, but pay was the clearest message of all, and he watched for the day when he could return to work.

If there is magic, or even only sleight-of-hand, the construction industry had its share of practitioners. Every square foot of reclaimed space in this new-old building was rentable. There wasn't a building code that dealt with this. Why would an inspector bother with this little mystery when there was a big concrete thing going up right next to it, hiding everything as it grew?

The renovated offices had an uncertain post-war charm, but the hoped-for trendy tenants didn't materialize, as the alleyway entrance was difficult to find, easy to miss, and the post office wouldn't recognize the address. The upper floors were never developed.

Eventually, an assortment of individual tenants occupied the suites on the first floor. The building's obscurity appealed to them and what little clientele they wanted. Visitors who did find the front door had to turn sharply around a corner to the elevator which faced a wall where the old lobby had been. There was no ground floor, and the only stairway was the metal fire escape at the back of the building, accessible through a narrow alley from the street behind–past a low, locked door in the foundation. Access to the first floor was via the cranky elevator, faithfully serviced from below by old Zoltan Zabç.

~

Meanwhile, the telephone company's administration systems were moving swiftly into the modern age. Hand-written ledgers had been replaced by punched cards by rolls of punched paper by rooms of magnetic tape by reams of computer print-outs that few eyes would ever read.

But one pair of eyes did notice something odd at

the end of a run, and their owner questioned it. Maintenance department's payroll ended with a code that none of the other departments used.

"What's this for?" the smart young college graduate asked. "Zed-Zed-a-b-c. What's that mean?"

"Let me see," the supervisor replied. "Hmm. Must be an old End Run code. It's redundant. Just delete it."

"Are you sure? It looks like there's pay attached to it, and a bank account. Should we check with HR?"

"Don't bother. It's likely just made up. I think I remember someone asking about that when we transferred everything to tape. It's nobody's name, obviously. Just an old code. Any undisbursed funds would have been cycled back into the system. Anyway, it's not enough money to even show up in an audit. Heck, nobody'd work for that pittance."

"Just delete it, then?"

"Yup. If that money really was going to someone, they'll holler when it stops. Then HR can check. That's easier than searching through thousands of records."

~

Zabç was relieved when deposits no longer appeared in his bank account. As low as the pay had been, he and his beloved had been thrifty and frugal. From day one of their happy life together, they saved diligently for a down-payment on a modest little house. They had burned the mortgage years ago.

He stopped attending the sub-basement when the tenants had all left and the elevator was quiet. He had never gone above to meet them, though he recognized their steps in the elevator car.

This time, the faux building was demolished for good, from the top to below ground.

He was grateful to be retired. His beloved had finally sold her shoe store, and they wanted to spend all their time together, maybe visit their grand-children.

Jan Fancy Hull

Acknowledgements

I am grateful to the Dear Readers, especially Margaret MacDonald Trites, who have read these stories over several years, murmuring encouragements as they picked out the grains of sand, gravel, or boulders I may have overlooked.

I am grateful to the judges in the Atlantic Writing Competition a decade ago who said the nicest things about these stories. There was no category for a collection of long short stories so I'd entered them all as a novel, fingers crossed. It didn't work, but one judge said, "I have a feeling you'll win out in the long run." Bless you. Such comments are nourishment that can keep a writer alive for years.

I am grateful to Moose House Publications for bringing these stories into the real world, and to editor Andrew Wetmore for making my good stories better. I *did* "win out".

I am grateful to the world and all the people in it for providing story ideas free for the picking.

I can't take the credit if I don't accept the blame: any errors are mine.

Jan Fancy Hull

About the author

Jan Fancy Hull, born on Nova Scotia's Eastern Shore, lives and writes beside (and sometimes on) a quiet lake in Lunenburg County. Jan engaged in various careers, enterprises, pursuits, and avocations, including as arts administrator, sailing tours skipper, and employee benefits broker.

Now retired (from earning a living) she writes and creates sculptures from Nova Scotia sandstone. She is a Member of the Writers Federation of Nova Scotia Writers' Council. She also likes to play golf, and drift on the lake in her small boat.

This is her second collection of short fiction.

Website: janfancyhull.ca
Facebook: Jan Fancy Hull

Teaser: The Church of Little Bo Peep and other stories

An excerpt from "Ten Questions", a short story included in The Church of Little Bo Peep and other stories, by Jan Fancy Hull

Albert stepped out into the service corridor. It was illuminated by very dim light emanating from the mall's centre court area. He looked down the long stretch past the stores, past the centre court and the big department store, to where he knew the busy liquor store anchored the other end. Not a freaking soul in sight. Every store closed, each sliding glass door slid shut, no lights inside.

The puzzle forming dimly in Albert MacLean's mind was this: it couldn't be night, because all the lights were off and he could still see, now that he wasn't in the men's. Also, it couldn't be dark outside, because if it was, the million-watt lights they had out there in the parking lot would be glaring into the mall brighter than day, not this grey light.

Albert looked behind him to check that the corridor to the dark washroom was still visible, and it was. It hadn't been much of a home, but in this moment he thought of it as a refuge. If it came to that.

No one could accuse Albert MacLean of being curious. Curiosity often called for bravery, often without warning, so it was his policy not to be curious. But Albert was curious now to learn what was the source of the odd light that brought dimness to the ends of the hallways.

He made his way toward the centre court, slowly, due to residual stiffness from his slumber in the stall, where, he remembered, he had propped his feet against the wall so a cursory inspection by a hasty janitor would not reveal his presence.

As he shuffled he became aware of another odd stimulus: sound.

Albert had not been treating himself all that well of late, or maybe too well. Whichever it was seemed to depend on who you were, and Albert had to be himself. The combination of analgesics he administered to himself sometimes made him less sharp than he might otherwise have been, kept him one remove from bright, shiny reality, like a protective coating over his nerves. Like wrapping a delicate rose in burlap against the harsh winter wind, as he liked to think of it.

Nothing wrong with that. Life was better, he found, when there was not too much of it. While the glitter and cacophony of a shopping mall might seem an odd refuge for one who wanted to deaden the senses, once Albert had acquired his "full metal jacket", as he thought of it, the mall seemed pretty, the piped-in music sounded delightful, the announcements to shoppers were messages to him from one who cared, the workers seemed like family and the regular shoppers like friends, and all of that felt better than the life of Albert MacLean that existed outside this place and outside his numbing drugs.

This new mall experience without the lights and without the noise was disorienting. The odd sound of which he was becoming aware was not Muzak, not announcements, not shopper-noises, but a dull, wide, urgent sort of sound, a sound that seemed to be paired with the grey light.

Some lights are paired with sounds, as Albert well knew. Ambulance sirens and revolving red lights, for instance.

Albert slowly approached the food court at the entrance to the Bedford River Mall. He would never have done what he did next had there been people watching, but there didn't seem to be any around. So he flattened his back against the wall as he had seen done on TV shows, and leaned out to reconnoiter around the corner. That didn't work, as Albert's neck was quite stiff and he couldn't turn his aching head far enough to see anything except what was in front of him. He flipped around, belly to the wall, and then allowed himself to peek at the source of light and sound.

"Ho-*ly*!" he said.

Had he seen the Rapture he wouldn't have been any more gob-smacked than at this moment.

The three-storey-high windows were inundated with a wide and steady fire-hose stream of water. That was the first thing he noticed, the water running down the glass and never letting up. The light that struggled through the layers of water and plate glass was mottled and uncertain. It seemed as though the flow would wash away the light. Or the glass itself. Albert had the sensation of being completely submerged *and* in a car-wash.

The water hitting the glass, that's what he had heard. Not a nice pit-a-pat rainy-day sound at all, but a nasty, dangerous crackling, like hail, like gravel shot from a car's continuously spinning tires. This wasn't rain. Rain falls down in drops. This was whole water. This was Biblical.

The usual array of twinkling, blinking, revolving, and flashing lights was gone from the mall. Not even any lights on the Spaceship in the food court. Albert loved to watch parents and grandparents resentfully dropping little kids into its cockpit while they enjoyed food court delicacies. Albert loved the tinny boom from the Spaceship's tiny speakers, the flash of lights as the Spaceship launched itself in a slow roll, the squeals (or screams) from the tiny tots. He felt he was one of the family, if only for that moment.

"Holy-moley," Albert said, for all the reasons that confronted him. Where were those over-indulging people now, and the servers who fried their fries?

Above and behind the roar of the waterfall, a very loud roar now that Albert was in front of the expanse of glass, was a siren sound. Albert had never heard anything like it, but he knew it was wind. Screaming wind.

"What the hell?" he whispered.

Albert moved farther into the centre court with no particular destination in mind, but it was instinctive to try a new perspective that would make things look right again. He wasn't going to even try the big, glass double doors against which so much water was being driven. He wasn't going to go through those doors into that weather, no way. Anyway, he knew rightly enough that they were locked, otherwise that wind would fling them wide open like a hyperactive Wal-Mart greeter.

An orange pylon slammed into the glass nearest Albert. He jumped back in fright, slipped, and fell. That's when he noticed that the wide terrazzo-tile floor was covered in water.

"Oh, fer cryin' out loud! Shit! Shit! Shit! Now look! Dammit!"

He was soaked all down his right side from his elbow to his pants and, he saw as he got himself up again, his sneakers.

Albert MacLean was not an especially fastidious fellow. But there was a line below which he tried not to sink in his present state of insulation from clarity, and being soaking wet and falling-down clumsy in public was below that line.

Albert was so accustomed to crowds here in the centre court that he was finding it difficult to keep in mind that he was alone. There really was nobody to see his sneakers filling up with the water draining from his pants, or his shoelaces afloat.

He looked around just to be sure of the nobody-ness. All he saw in the flat wavy light was a pool of water, spreading not all that slowly from the front doors, where he noticed it spraying in through the gaps. The flood was heading across the court toward the locked doors and brand-new carpet of the big department store.

"Holy," Albert said again. After a moment's reflection the imminent implication of this situation dawned on him and he said, "Better look out, ya dweeb!"

The big department store's manager was a weiner who had given his security staff strict orders to keep Albert MacLean from setting one toe on that carpet. Albert had never misbehaved in the store, had taken nothing of any value from it, had even sometimes straightened up the mess on the shelves since the little pinch-faced bastard wouldn't hire enough staff to look after the store. But one day the little shit had loudly called Albert a vagrant and booted him out.

Albert's friends at the coffee shop in the food court saw and heard, and Albert was ashamed, but they called him over and gave him a large double-double on the house and kept checking on him until he had calmed down.

He was no vagrant. Albert's inheritance meant never having to say he was sorry. Well, no, it meant never having to ask for handouts; he was sorry about a lot of things that his inheritance couldn't help him with. He had been and said sorry a lot before he found those pills.

"Keep that water off your fancy carpet, why dontcha, you little piss-ant!" Albert said to the locked glass doors, to his own moderated amusement. It was funny, but not that funny right now, standing as he was in inch-deep water, alone, in the middle of the Bedford River Mall centre court.

Want to find out what happens next? *The Church of Little Bo Peep and other stories* is available from your local bookseller or directly from moosehousepress.com.

www.ingramcontent.com/pod-product-compliance
Lightning Source LLC
Chambersburg PA
CBHW070508200726
48293CB00007B/2443